KISS ME AT MIDNIGHT

THE KISSING TEST SERIES BOOK 3

MELINDA CURTIS

D1738274

ACKNOWLEDGMENTS

Some books are fun to write – a wild ride from start to finish. This book wasn't one of them. Born after a move from California to Oregon, nurtured during a pandemic quarantine, and surviving through a remodel where too many walls were knocked down and a kitchen was removed. This book would not have been possible without the love and occasional kicks in the pants from my family, one of my team (Diane Bryant), and one of my critique partners (Cari Lynn Webb). They gave Granny Dotty more antics than I thought possible and made sure that Lily had the heart and moral fiber I've come to expect from a Summer sister. Special thanks to Victoria Cooper for her inspired cover design. It's hard not to have fun writing with covers like these.

Here's to more Summer sister romances helped along by Grandma Dotty...just...please. Not during a renovation and quarantine.

PROLOGUE

Dotty Summer had a bucket list, and her son Tim wasn't happy with it.

"Mom, if you know where Lily disappeared to last night, you need to tell me because I heard..." Tim didn't finish his sentence. He paced across Dotty's blue and gold Turkish rug in her mother-in-law quarters at his New York home, scraping the soles of his Italian loafers on all that fine wool.

If I hadn't taken a twenty-four-hour vow of silence, I'd tell him to take his shoes off or pick up his feet.

That vow of silence was on Dotty's bucket list. She'd created the list because she was afraid her mind was slipping gears a few times too often and new experiences were said to stimulate the brain. She'd already filled some buckets–visiting a gator farm, touring the Everglades, dating a younger man. But she had plenty of things remaining on her list, not to mention she enjoyed adding to it.

Tim thought her bucket list was ridiculous (he'd read it without her permission). Not breaking stride, her middle-aged son ran a hand through his hair. It was still dark brown and shiny. He covered his grays the same way he covered up the aging process–with help. "I heard Lily left the fundraiser last night with a man."

And me.

Dotty smirked. Her son didn't know everything.

"Lily is so gullible when it comes to helping others," Tim said ruefully. "And now she's mixed up in something that'll ruin her."

What?

Given Lily was an elected state representative who prided herself on a squeaky-clean reputation, that gave Dotty pause. She frowned, mentally reviewing what she remembered of last night's events. Tim, she decided, was overreacting.

"Lily isn't answering her phone." Tim turned and paced back, dragging his feet once more. "She's been so respon-sible lately, unlike Kitty or Aubrey, who've been letting their emotions get the better of them."

Fallen in love, he meant.

If it weren't for this vow of silence...

Dotty was a firm believer in the power of true love. She pressed her lips together to keep from giving her son a piece of her mind.

Tim had five daughters, all of whom he loved *condi-tionally*–no "un" attached. That fact alone might have made Dotty over-react more than a time or two to support those young women, most of whom were now in their thirties. Add all the mistakes Tim had made in his nearly forty-year marriage and his borderline shady business dealings, and... Well, Dotty hadn't stopped loving him. He was one of her children, after all. But that didn't mean Tim couldn't annoy her. Take right now, for instance. He'd woken her up before seven. And she'd been in the midst of the darndest dream, one where she'd been rushing to someone's rescue, felling villains with one blow. *Ka-pow!*

Dotty allowed herself a small smile.

"Lily didn't answer her door when I buzzed her apartment thirty minutes ago." Tim smoothed his tie without breaking stride across her Turkish rug.

Dotty cinched her pink chenille robe tight, which was the only thing keeping her from grabbing onto Tim's tie and pulling him to a halt. Didn't he know how important this rug was to her? It had been a gift for her fiftieth wedding anniversary. A widow cherished a good husband's gifts.

Tim stomped by on another pass. "Please, Mom... If you know anything... Please forget this stupid vow of silence and tell me. Lily's about to do something she'll regret."

Dotty wasn't sure that was true. But she needed time to think about this. She scribbled a note and held it up so Tim could read it: *Stop pacing, please.*

Tim came to a stop and peered at the note. "Stop racing peas? Stop racing peas?"

He's misunderstanding me on purpose.

Grinding her bridge work in frustration, Dotty pointed at Tim's loafers.

He crossed his arms over his chest and stared down at her without one single ounce of respect for Dotty or her carpet. "One little mistake...One public misstep...And Lily's political career will be ruined." He tsked. "And all before I had a chance to reap the benefits of her position."

And there it was. The real reason for Tim's concern. Nepotism.

Dotty came to her feet and steered her middle-aged son toward the door.

"Mom, what are you doing? You know something, don't you? Break your vow of silence. You're not a nun."

Mouth firmly closed, Dotty bustled her son out the door and slammed it behind him.

"*Mom!*"

As soon as the lock clicked into place, Dotty began to worry about Lily and handsome actors with angelic voices. Anyone with an over-abundance of self-ambition was a watch-out in her book. And actors... Well, they were about as trustworthy as reality TV stars.

"Ah, nuts." Dotty opened her closet and reached for her travel bag, giving up on a day of silence in favor of a day seeking peace of mind.

1

Seven and a half hours ago...

Lily Summer leaned against the back wall at her younger sister Aubrey's animal rescue fundraiser and sighed. Aubrey had just received a very public, very romantic marriage proposal. A receiving line had formed in the New York City ballroom.

"I know that look." Lily's twin sister Violet elbowed Lily. "Happy and envious."

"You've got the same *always a bridesmaid* look on your face," Lily guessed. She wasn't wearing her glasses so she couldn't be sure. "You should date more."

Violet and Lily were identical twins, but their styles were completely different. Lily wore a conservative black cocktail dress, low heels, and had her brown hair in a bun. Violet wore a flirty yellow cocktail dress and matching sparkly flats. Her long brown, highlighted hair spilled over her shoulders.

"I don't have time to date. But you..." Vi curled her arm around Lily's waist and gave her a side-hug. "You should find a regular man. No more three date rule."

"Your concern is noted and tabled." As a junior state congresswoman, dating was awkward for Lily. Given her political career path—she wanted to be the first female mayor of New York City—searching for love seemed too much of a risk in this kiss-and-tell culture. Add to that an uncomfortable incident in her past, and three dates was her limit. "I'm in fund-raising mode. Hot Meals and Shelter is at risk of closing." It was a vital soup kitchen, food bank, and shelter in her district. "And I have to start thinking about courting donors for my re-election campaign." Her least favorite activity.

"You always have an emergency or a pressing need." Dropping her arm, Vi stared out over the crowd. "I'm all for public service but not public servitude. I can't remember the last time you mentioned going out with friends, much less on a date. Get a life."

"I'm here, aren't I?" But Vi had a point. Lily's friendship circle had begun shrinking fifteen years ago until now the only people she seemed to socialize with were her family.

Violet nudged Lily again. "Hey, is that Rachel Cohen over there by the stage?"

Lily squinted, debating whether to put her glasses on or not. The crowd parted. The redhead in question certainly dressed like Rachel, a reality TV star and their former child-hood friend. She wore a clingy burgundy gown with a slit above the thigh. She hung on to a tuxedoed man who had to be seven feet tall. "It might be Rachel. I don't remember her husband being that tall though."

Vi tsked. "Don't tell me you haven't heard that Rachel dumped her husband of thirty days for that basketball player? Paulo Silva almost got cut last season from the New Jersey Badgers until he started dating Rachel." The Badgers were the NBA's latest expansion team. Violet was an avid fan. "I thought they'd trade him when Rachel dumped him and married Michael Huston. But here we are, almost a year later. And Paulo's contract is up for negotiation."

Lily nodded. "Notoriety sells in Hollywood and the NBA." Tickets, jerseys, and endorsement deals.

"Are you talking about Rachel?" Grandma Dotty appeared out of nowhere. Her petite frame and delicate features made her look fragile. But she had game when her mind was clear. She leaned in closer and said in a conspiratorial voice, "Everybody's talking about Rachel. And why wouldn't they? She's a pip on *Slaying the Upper East Side!*" Grandma Dotty always grinned when talking about her guilty pleasure. "Since you two grew up with Rachel, you know she's got a big heart beneath that bad girl exterior."

Lily refrained from comment.

Grandma Dotty didn't notice. "Too bad her marriage didn't work out. Michael was just using her fame to build his business. I saw through him from the moment they met in Season Eight, Episode Four."

"Everyone's avoiding that pip like the plague," Vi said absently. And then she turned abruptly to face Lily. "Let's go over and say hello."

"No." Lily sucked in a breath.

"Hot diggity. Let's do it. Maybe I'll get her autograph." Never one to hesitate, Grandma Dotty high-tailed it over.

Violet stared at Lily with raised brows.

"I feel for what she's going through, Vi. Really I do," Lily said quickly. "But don't ask me to talk to her." Rachel could be the happy-go-lucky, life of the party and then throw you under the bus. Lily didn't want to get run over again. "I wish her all the best."

Vi took Lily by both arms. "Repeat after me, Lily Roselind Summer. Rachel doesn't have the power to hurt me. I am a bigger person than she is." Vi hesitated, and then plowed on, "And I deserve love. The slow-growing, long-lasting, forever kind of love that comes from more than three dates. Nothing Rachel can say or do will change that."

"I know." And yet, uncertainty gripped Lily with cowardly claws. It had been fifteen years since Rachel had abandoned her in a sketchy situation. Lily hadn't talked to her since. Nor had she seriously dated anyone. "You go and greet Rachel. Tell her...Tell her hi for me."

"You're so brave everywhere else." Shaking her head, Vi dropped her hold on Lily and left her propped against the back wall.

Vi's right. I need a change.

Perhaps after the next election.

A waiter stopped in front of Lily. "Ma'am?"

Ma'am? Lily fought to keep from frowning.

No one should be allowed to call a thirty-two-year-old woman *ma'am*. It made Lily want to go home and search her hairline for grays. *Geez. Ma'am?*

"The man at the bar asked me to give you this." The waiter handed Lily a business card.

In the darkened section of the ballroom and without her glasses on, there was no way Lily could read what was printed on the front, much less scribbled on the back, of that card. She thanked the young server anyway, shoving it into her clutch with her cell phone.

It was probably from one of her constituents. Someone who needed a new sidewalk in front of their brownstone or wanted to complain about the high rate they paid for garbage.

Just in case the man at the bar was someone who could

advance her career or find her true love, Lily waved in the general direction of the bar. And then she stifled a yawn.

Just a few more minutes, and then she'd wish Aubrey well on her engagement to an Ecuadorian hunk and make her way home. Tomorrow was a workday, after all.

"Lily." A man appeared next to her. He was tall, dark haired, and smelled like a sunny day at the Hamptons.

She almost reached inside her clutch for her glasses so she could see what he looked like.

"Thanks for agreeing to talk." He slid his arm around her waist and guided her toward the door and the hotel lobby.

And she let him because it was loud in the New York City ballroom and her feet hurt in her heels.

"I need some air," potentially hunky man was saying. His voice was warm, almost familiar in her ear. His hand was warm, almost familiar on her hip. His name though... His name was still a mystery.

I should put on my glasses.

It was just that she'd been raised as a New York City socialite and had four sisters who had excellent vision and were beautiful. She always felt dumpy in her glasses, and contacts bothered her eyes.

Pride. The downfall of most politicians.

I'm allowed one vice.

But she was curious about the man beside her.

Lily fumbled with her clutch as he swept her toward the lobby entrance where a loud crowd seemed to have formed. Her escort slowed as he led her out into the brisk spring evening. And as he slowed, the crowd erupted in squeals of excitement. Suited security guards held back the surge.

"I didn't expect this." Her escort's voice was deep. His

words well-modulated. He had no Brooklyn accent or swagger.

"I need a ride, Lily. Can you drop me off?" Grandma Dotty inserted herself between Lily and the man, craning her neck to stare up into his face. "Well, hello, Trouble. I'm Dotty, Lily's grandmother. I loved you in *The Music Man.*"

"Thank you." Lily's escort waved to the throng.

The crowd screamed louder. Cameras and phones flashed.

Apparently, he was famous. Perhaps an actor. The probability of him needing help to fight city hall increased.

Grandma Dotty mimicked his wave. "I never knew animal rescue societies had such a big fan base." She was completely oblivious to the likelihood that the crowd was here to see Lily's mystery man. "Give generously!" She blew kisses.

Lily loved her grandmother, but she wasn't as sharp as she used to be.

Lily slid her glasses on and glanced up at her escort. Her very handsome, very buff escort. "Judson Hambly?" The actor who'd been her teenage crush? The actor who was currently starring as a superhero in a television show? He looked like he could do his own stunts, like they didn't have to pad his supersuit with a fake six-pack.

Several teenage girls screamed louder, presumably at the confirmation of the name of the hunky actor, or because he smoothly switched positions with Dotty and settled a proprietary hand on Lily's hip once more.

"Your car is ready." The gold buttons on a hotel attendant's burgundy uniform gleamed in the bright lights as he opened the rear door to a black Town Car.

Lily hadn't seen her car drive up. She moved toward it anyway, shocked by Judson's continued presence at her side.

"Are you two dating?" someone shouted.

"Kiss her!" someone else demanded as Dotty gingerly got in the back seat.

"What's going on?" Suspicious of his motives, Lily's gaze searched Judson's. *Is he going to kiss me?* Her heart raced.

"I need a ride out of here." Judson's blue eyes were electric but held no heat promising kisses.

Lily was...relieved? At least, she should be. She'd built her career on practically being invisible in a city that celebrated celebrity.

But still... The seed was planted: *What would it be like to kiss Judson Hambly?*

Unbidden, a thought arose: *Marvelous.*

A little bell went off in Lily's head. It was the bell that used to ring when she and Violet were teenagers and snuck out at night seeking mischief. Lily's heart pounded faster and her lips curved upward. She hadn't tripped that alarm in what seemed like forever.

Because of what happened with Rachel.

Lily's smile fell. She got in the car, and then slid over, making room for Judson.

"Buckle up, Mr. Superstar." Grandma Dotty snapped her seat belt in place. "Ryan likes to speed late at night."

Lily put on the center seat belt and then fussed with the hem of her black cocktail dress before risking a glance at the man who'd whisked her away from the party.

Judson Hambly was as handsome in person as on movie and TV screens, even doing something as basic as snapping his seat belt.

He probably doesn't appreciate being stared at like eye candy.

Lily carefully modulated her expression and tried to look at him the way she would one of her political colleagues. "Where can we drop you?"

"I…" Judson suddenly seemed at a loss for words.

"Ms. Summer." Ryan caught her eye in the rear-view mirror, interrupting Judson's answer. "Nina wants you to check your email." Nina was Lily's assistant. "Something requires your urgent attention before midnight. She marked it time sensitive and provided me with the address if you're interested."

"That's odd." Lily took her cell phone out of her purse and scrolled through her messages. She opened a forwarded email from Nina with "time sensitive" in the subject line and scanned through the missive quickly. It was from Abe Cohen, Rachel's father. When Lily got to the end, she gasped, "No." It was a complete Godsend of an offer, but he mentioned needing a favor in return.

Quid pro quo. The downfall of many a politician.

"What's the matter?" Dotty peered at Lily's cell phone. "Is it another marriage proposal?"

"No." It was an offer to fund Hot Meals and Shelter. "Ryan, we're going to need that address. Let's drop off the other passengers first."

"It's eleven-thirty, Ms. Summer." Ryan pointed at the clock in the dashboard as he accelerated. "I won't be able to drop off Mrs. Summer in that timeframe. And we have yet to discuss where to drop Mr. Hambly."

Judson cleared his throat. "I – "

"What's going on, Lily?" Grandma Dotty cut off Judson's reply and grabbed Lily's arm. "I've seen *Law & Order*. No legitimate business transaction is made at this time of night."

She was right, of course. And there was that incident with Rachel from fifteen years ago that made this feel even murkier.

But the clock was ticking on keeping the food bank

open. Offers like this one didn't come along every day. And it expired in twenty-eight minutes.

Why did it expire in twenty-eight minutes?

"I have to take this meeting." Lily had to know what kind of strings were attached to the deal. She looked at Judson. "I hate to do this but... Can we drop you here?"

"No." Jud hadn't come this far to be tossed out at a corner. Lily Summer was exactly what he was looking for. All he had to do was find the right moment to ask her out.

Jud leaned forward until he caught Dotty's eye. "Clearly, Lily needs backup at this meeting."

"Yes, indeedy, she does." Dotty played right into Jud's hands. "Are you sweet on my granddaughter, Judson? She could be Marion the Librarian to your Harold Hill." A *Music Man* reference.

"I'd like that." Jud gave Lily a good-natured smile. He'd gone to the animal rescue benefit tonight because his agent had told him the attendees were upper-crust New Yorkers, staid creatures that were miles apart from Jud and his Hollywood ways.

As a popular star of film and TV, Jud had spent the last decade snubbing his nose at the Hollywood power players, choosing instead to play the field with a string of beautiful women. And now that he wanted to transition to directing film, he was finding his image was in need of repair. It wouldn't have mattered if he'd had a trust fund or inherited some of the Hambly billions. If that were the case, he could have financed his own film. Too late, he'd realized he should have been brown-nosing. No one was interested in gambling one hundred, fifty, or even twenty million dollars on the directorial debut of a playboy who shunned the Hollywood establishment, even if he was well-pedigreed in the acting community.

As part of his image-repair plan, Jud was in need of a part-time girlfriend, someone who was above reproach and didn't require much of his time. A fake girlfriend, to be exact. He'd sat at the bar all night grilling the knowledge-able bartender about the single ladies in attendance. Enter Representative Lily Summer.

His gaze drifted toward the woman who sat next to him. Her warm thigh brushed his every time the driver made a left turn. She was businesslike and reserved. Her official website pictures showed her in glasses with her brown hair in an uninspired bun. In the photos, she dressed well, if somewhat unimaginatively, like she had tonight. Pantsuits. Dresses with simple lines.

A willowy body like hers could pull off more feminine looks, a high hemline, a bare midriff, a bikini where less was more. He glanced at Lily's feet and added sexier shoes to the list.

Lily Summer doesn't need sexy shoes to be sexy.

That thought struck out of the blue. Jud shook his head. He wanted to date Lily, not fall in love.

"If you must come, you'll wait in the car," Lily said in a calm, collected manner.

He liked her composure. She'd be unflustered in front of the media. Another plus for the role he wanted her to play.

"We're not waiting in the car." Diminutive Dotty sat up tall in the seat as she dug through her purse. "Besides, you can't leave me behind. I have the mace." She pulled out a small cannister. Her finger moved toward the pump trigger as if she were about to mace someone.

Fast as lightning, Lily claimed the mace before disaster struck and Dotty sprayed the driver.

Add calm in unexpected situations to the list of Lily's good attributes. She could handle the limelight. She was perfect for the role of Judson Hambly's girlfriend.

"Okay, you can hold my mace," Dotty allowed. "But I'm still coming along."

Lily sighed.

They took another left at speed. Lily's body pressed against Jud's.

Increasingly, Jud wondered what it would be like to hold Lily in his arms and kiss her.

"I'm coming, too," Jud told Lily. "We've got your back."

"Now tell your supersquad where we're going." Dotty was the perfect foil for the situation.

Lily sighed. "Abe Cohen wants to give generously to the primary food kitchen and shelter in my district."

"Abe Cohen has serious money," Jud blurted. He owned several companies and had stakes in several sports teams, including the New Jersey Badgers.

"You know him?" Lily asked sharply.

Jud nodded. "After I did *The Music Man*, he paid me to perform at his daughter Rachel's birthday celebration." The very wealthy often booked the very famous to attend their private functions. His performance had been filmed for the reality show Rachel starred in.

"I was going to ask my family to book you for my birthday, Judson." Dotty had a faraway look in her eyes. "It's on my bucket list. I have a wonderful voice and love *The Music Man*." She burst into song, *"Seventy six trombones–"*

The driver took a hard, unexpected left, which sent Lily's soft, warm body careening into Jud's.

She can careen into me anytime.

"If you know Abe, I don't think you should be my wing-man," Lily was saying to Jud underneath the warbly notes Dotty was singing.

"...*a hundred and ten coronets—*"

"On the contrary, I think it will help." Not that Jud knew how it possibly could, but if Abe was in the mood to spend, he might invest in Jud's movie. Everybody knew social settings smoothed the way for business deals.

"...*followed by rows and rows...*"

To avoid additional argument, Jud joined Dotty in the signature song, bringing a smile to the old woman's face.

"It's too bad you weren't in *Les Misérables*," Dotty told Jud when they'd finished. "We could have sung *One Day More*. Although now that you wear superhero tights, you probably don't want to do more on Broadway."

"We're here," Ryan said before Jud could contradict Dotty's assumption. "Twenty minutes, Ms. Summer." He slowed the car, turned into the basement parking lot of a high-rise building, and stopped next to a VIP elevator.

"I can handle this on my own," Lily said, but she sounded uncertain.

"We're coming with you anyway," Jud insisted.

"Yup," Dotty seconded.

Everyone got out. Lily entered a code from her email into the security pad and the VIP elevator doors slid open. They got into the elevator and rode toward the top floor.

Lily turned to Jud. "Why did you want to talk to me tonight?"

"I bet he wanted to ask you out," Dotty said knowingly. "You're just his type."

"Ha!" Lily gave a shout of laughter. "I am nothing like the women Judson dates."

That was then...

Jud gritted his teeth. "Actually, it's Jud. And I *was* going to ask you on a date."

"You weren't." Lily smoothed a wisp of brown hair back toward her bun. "You were going to ask me to help you rezone your brownstone."

The elevator doors slid open before Jud could argue.

Actually, it's Jud. And I was *going to ask you on a date.*

Despite not believing him, a thrill shot through Lily. She hadn't had many thrills since she'd graduated college and begun working in public service.

The open elevator doors began to close, bringing her back to reality and her ambitions. There was no room in her career plan for mooning over handsome actors, not even ones who held elevator doors for her.

"White and gold," Dotty spoke reverently, looking around as she stepped out of the elevator. "It's like I've died and gone to heaven. I haven't, have I?"

"No," Jud reassured her.

The Cohen family foyer was white marble with gold light fixtures. Whoever had designed the place had gone overboard. White marble covered the floor, went up the walls, and across the ceiling. It screamed: *We have money. Lots of it.*

"Someone's redecorated since I've been here last," Lily whispered, struck by how different it looked. "Back then the foyer was covered in red velvet wallpaper."

Bordello wallpaper, Rachel had jokingly called it.

"I prefer the red velvet," Dotty whispered, touching the marble wall and adding, "I used to play canasta with Abe's mother. Back then this had yellow paneling."

The Summer women turned to Jud as if expecting him to add to the conversation.

"I've never been here. I performed at their Hamptons house." Jud tilted his head, studying Lily with those bright blue eyes and grinning. "Why do you think I wouldn't ask you out?"

Lily's pulse raced with excitement. Jud made her feel the opposite of boring.

The front door opened, saving her from answering.

"Mr. Cohen will join you shortly." A rather non-descript old man with a shaved head escorted them to a darkly paneled library and closed the door behind them.

A French rococo clock marked fifteen minutes before midnight.

"You didn't answer my question," Jud said gently, moving closer to Lily.

She adjusted her black glasses and tried to tell herself that she felt warm all over because she hadn't talked to Rachel since that one disastrous night years ago. It was apprehension making her heart pound, not attraction.

"I love interrogations." Dotty grabbed hold of a standing floor lamp and tilted it so that the light blinded Lily. "It's cat and mouse, the best part of any cop show. Answer the question."

"Whose side are you on?" Lily held up a hand to block the light from her eyes.

"Yours if you'll confess, see." Grandma Dotty tried to imitate Jimmy Cagney, one of her favorite old school actors.

"What do I have to confess?" Lily squinted in the light.

"That you'd love to go out with this handsome man, but only if he wears his superhero duds." Her grandmother giggled.

"The network doesn't let the superhero suit off the lot," Jud said good-naturedly, adding in a suggestive tone, "Although I have an in with the costume designer and have been known to wear it to paid private events."

Private. A bedroom came to mind.

Lily's mouth went dry as she imagined Jud standing at the foot of her bed in his superhero duds. And then her brain registered another word: *paid.* Without a paycheck, it was unlikely Jud would don his superhero suit for her.

"Well that settles it," Lily said in a voice she hoped dispelled all argument. "I don't pay for dates, even if I'd be impressed by the supersuit."

"Point taken." Grandma Dotty set the lamp back upright and moved on to rifle through a small desk next to it.

"Don't snoop." Lily couldn't believe Jud was still staring at her, couldn't believe she was blushing. She squared her shoulders. "If you aren't going to be straight with me about wanting to meet me, Jud, I'll just guess. I bet you wanted to talk because your neighbor leaves out his trash cans all week." Complaints about neighbors were surprisingly high in her district.

"Nope." Jud crossed his arms over his broad chest. "I wanted to–"

"Don't tell me." Lily narrowed her eyes. "The brownstone you want to remodel is zoned multi-family?" That was another popular issue with her constituents.

"Nope."

"*Aha!*" Dotty pulled a slim black cord from a drawer, jiggling it until the plug swung free. "You can't find these flip phone chargers anymore. I'm taking it." She proceeded to tie the cord around her waist like a belt. "Abe owes me."

"Put that back, please." Lily's command was spoken without significantly shifting her attention from Jud. "I can get you a new cell phone charger."

"Not like this, you can't." Grandma Dotty held the plug in her hand. "They don't make flip phones like mine or the charger anymore. And before I forget, I want my mace back."

"Dad wouldn't approve of you having mace."

"Your father doesn't approve of me, regardless." Grandma Dotty's chin took on a mutinous tilt.

Jud chuckled as if he found this tremendously amusing. He wouldn't laugh if Grandma Dotty accidentally maced him.

"Lily, Dotty, and...Jud." Abe charged into the room with all the energy of an uncapped fire plug. He had short black hair that was teased straight up and wore a blue silk shirt over gray slacks. "Thank you so much for agreeing to meet with me. I'm under a tight timeline." Abe sat down in a brown leather club chair, signaling to his assistant to close the door and stay outside. His gaze took in Grandma Dotty and her cell phone charger belt with only a brief quirk to his brow.

Lily decided it was late and time to get down to business. "About your offer to donate to the Hot Meals and Shelter..."

"In exchange for a favor." Abe was looking speculatively at Jud, not Lily.

"What favor?" Jud moved beside Lily and draped his arm around her waist, resting that big hand of his on her hip.

Grandma Dotty glanced at Jud, at his hand, and then she

sidled up on the other side of him and draped his arm over her shoulder. "Yeah, what favor?"

"Could it be that you haven't heard?" Abe had a salesman's smile, big enough to hold all his agendas. "Rachel was recently granted a quickie divorce from her groom of thirty days."

"That was the best episode all season," Grandma Dotty said in all earnestness. "I record them all on my VCR."

The clock ticked closer to midnight. Lily was acutely aware that Abe's donation deal was about to expire, almost as acutely as she was aware of every inch of Jud's hot body touching hers.

Violet was right. I do need to date.

Abe's brow wrinkled. "Yes, well. To stave off bad press, Rachel wants to get married immediately to her true love and put all the negative talk behind her."

"Not so fast, Abe," Grandma Dotty said sagely. "I know how these shows work. You'd get higher ratings if she'd ditch Paulo for a third man." She stared up at Jud. "We've got your third man right here."

"I'm not available to play the part of the third wheel. I'm in a relationship." Jud spoke like a man in love, staring at Lily like she was the object of all that love.

Be still my heart...

"I'm sorry Rachel's going through such a hard time," Lily began in her most business-like tone of voice. "But my priority is for Hot Meals and Shelter–"

"We'll get to that." Abe brushed her concerns aside. "Rachel has missed you, Lily."

Lily stiffened, unintentionally moving closer to Jud. Rachel didn't miss Lily. Rachel hadn't contacted Lily since stranding her in the dead of night. "I'm not here to revisit the past. I can tell you more about Hot Meals and Shelter.

We currently feed over one thousand families a day, both at a community center and through weekly donations of groceries. And we offer shelter to close to two hundred women and children."

"That's something to be proud of," Jud said softly.

"Lily cares about people," Grandma Dotty chimed in.

"You three seem to be on the same page, which is perfect." Abe rubbed his hands together, staring at them in a way that made Lily nervous. "Rachel is in need of friendly faces at her wedding this week and–"

"Stop right there, Mr. Cohen." Jud stared down at Lily with what seemed like love in his eyes. "My girlfriend and I can't attend."

Lily stared up at Jud. "*My–?*"

"Love. *My love*," Jud repeated quickly. He took Lily's hand, threading their fingers together. "We've only just begun using the L-word. We've been keeping things quiet between us. I don't think we're ready for the media scrutiny."

He loves me? Lily was temporarily struck speechless as her heart melted.

And then her brain kicked into gear: *It's an act. He's an actor. We've only just met.*

And yet, Lily's smaller hand fit nicely in his and the warmth of him next to her momentarily stole all other thoughts from her head. And she should be thinking about– about personal space and safety. Her gaze drifted to the door. At the very least, she should be protecting her professional reputation. The path to re-election wasn't paved with fake relationships with hunky actors or wedding attendance for grudge-bearing reality TV stars. She had to put a stop to this.

And I will. On the count of three.

Lily drew a deep breath.

On the count of three, I'll redirect Abe to Hot Meals and Shelter.

One.

Two.

Jud drew Lily in for a kiss that knocked her mental train of thought completely off its rails. He kissed her hard and fast and when he drew back Lily was breathless.

Oh, my.

He kept that strong arm around her as the clock in the room chimed midnight.

Midnight. How fitting. At any moment Lily expected to turn into a pumpkin. She adjusted her glasses and cleared her throat, feeling her cheeks flame with heat.

"Oh, my." Grandma Dotty fanned herself with her hand.

"Young love. I get it. But you'll have to go public sometime," Abe told them. "And I'm in desperate need of wedding guests with impeccable reputations who–"

"Impeccable reputations?" Releasing Jud, Lily laughed. She couldn't help it. All that Abe-induced stress and kiss-fueled adrenaline needed an outlet. "And you thought of the Summers? Have you forgotten my younger sister Maggie was jilted at the altar and her fiancé claims to have fallen in love with my older sister Kitty? Or that my cousin Tiffany had a string of discarded fiancés before she finally got married? When it comes to families without scandals in their closet, it's not the Summers." It was the truth, but she'd say anything to bow out of this wedding invitation. "It's after midnight. We're tired. Cut to the chase, Abe."

Jud and Grandma Dotty nodded in agreement.

"I'd forgotten how blunt you can be." Some of the energy seemed to drain from Abe. "Rachel plans to have a small wedding on our yacht Friday, which leaves port for

Miami tomorrow morning. But it's not a happy time for her. All her wedding invitations have been turned down, even by the castmates on her TV show. She's taken it very hard."

For the first time that evening, Lily felt sorry for Rachel.

"She's my little girl," Abe went on in a near-broken voice. "I want to help her, but she's shut me out. I just turned sixty. I know I don't understand your generation, but I need someone to help her see how jumping from relationship to relationship isn't the answer. The answer is family. Me." He choked up. "I know what you're thinking. How can you help? You and Rachel haven't talked in forever. But you used to be best friends. I think you can help Rachel realize she should cancel the wedding. My hope is that a break from all this foolishness will open the door to a better relationship for me and Rachel."

"I'm not following how your goals for Rachel have anything to do with Hot Meals and Shelter." Lily crossed her arms over her chest.

Grandma Dotty mirrored her stance. "Same."

Jud frowned. "It sounds like Abe wants you to talk Rachel out of getting married in exchange for...a donation?"

Their host nodded.

"There's no chance I can stop Rachel's wedding." Lily shook her head. "Jud has higher odds of blocking the nuptials by stealing Rachel from Paulo."

"You leave Paulo to me," Grandma Dotty said with a toss of her head. "Men find me irresistible."

"It's your singing voice," Jud deadpanned, causing Grandma Dotty to beam.

"Hey." Abe snapped his fingers several times to get their attention. "I'm serious, folks. In her quest to be the most dramatic ratings-grabber, Rachel has lost sight of what it's like to live a real life away from the cameras. I know she doesn't love Paulo. He's just her...her...her boy toy." Abe grimaced. "I'm willing to pay someone to help me reel her back in. If you stop the proceedings, Lily, I'll sponsor Hot Meals and Shelter in its entirety for one year."

Lily gasped. Just last week she'd told the director of Hot Meals and Shelter that she'd do anything to keep the charity open. The organization was near and dear to Lily's heart. But that bold statement Lily had made to the director was now being put to the test. Was she willing to risk hurt to feed and shelter thousands in need?

Grandma Dotty gave her a speculative look.

"And for my daughter's favorite actor..." Abe rubbed his jaw as he considered Jud. "If you help stop the wedding, I'll back your directorial debut by investing twenty-five percent of your film's budget. You're working with twenty million, right?"

Jud drew back. "How did you know I wanted to direct? Or the size of my budget? I haven't told anyone but my agent."

"And he, in turn, put out feelers with several producers." Abe settled back in his chair like a man certain he was about to win a poker match. "I'm plugged into the entertainment industry. My father used to own several theaters on Broadway. And I made my first million producing scaffolding for use in construction and entertainment production. People have been talking for months about you seeking financial backing for a small film with big heart."

Jud frowned.

"What do I get?" Grandma Dotty tightened the power cord around her waist. "I'm worth something."

"You're not going," Lily blurted. It was bad enough that she was considering Abe's proposal. She didn't want her grandmother involved in this.

Abe didn't miss a beat. "You get a berth on my luxury yacht, Dotty. You'd like that, wouldn't you? I once heard you tell my mother you'd love to sail on *My Private Dancer*."

Grandma Dotty's forehead puckered. "Your mother's been dead five years."

"I have the memory of an elephant." Abe tapped his temple. "And in case you're thinking my pride and joy is outdated, I just upgraded her last summer with Rachel's design help. All one hundred and eighty-six feet of her."

"Grandma Dotty's not going," Lily said again, louder this time and directly to Abe.

"Fine. Just you two lovebirds then. What do you say?" Abe cracked his knuckles one-by-one, adding to the tension in the room. "Will you help me?"

Lily's stomach knotted. Her wounded teenage self said no. The humanitarian in her said yes. She turned toward Jud to break the tie.

That Hollywood hunk stared deeply into Lily's eyes, as if to say he'd do it if she did, as if he truly had her back.

For a moment, Lily could imagine she and Jud as a couple. They both came from prominent, wealthy families. They both had demanding careers. They wouldn't date so frequently that they'd suffocate each other. The press would dub them with one of those ridiculously cute monikers that was a result of combining their names, like Judlily or Lilyson.

Lily rolled her eyes. This was so not her. Where were her sisters and the Kissing Test when she needed them? They'd developed the test as a way to weed out fortune hunters and bad boys. In Lily's experience, men who kissed women they'd just met–no matter how skillfully–were a caution. Judson Hambly had dated more women than Leonardo DiCaprio. And if Lily went through with Abe's scheme, there was a high probability that the world would add her to the list of his conquests.

"I can see you still have doubts, Lily." Abe was back to smiling and rubbing his hands together. "If you're thinking Rachel won't want you on this trip, rest assured. I talked to her about inviting you before she left for the fundraiser tonight. She gave me her blessing. The past is just water under the bridge."

Easy for Rachel to say. She was the one who'd saved herself and left Lily in danger.

Everyone stared at Lily, waiting for her decision.

"It sounds like an adventure." Grandma Dotty pouted. "Do what you like, Lily. It's not like you don't leave me behind all the time on your adventures."

Lily couldn't remember the last time she'd been on an adventure.

"Do what's right," Jud murmured in her ear.

"What's right is..." Lily began, trailing off when Jud took her hand once more. She stared up into those blue eyes, which was a mistake. He made her feel wanted. He made her want to agree just to stay by his side.

"We'll do it, won't we?" Jud murmured. "We'll stop Rachel from making another mistake?"

Lily nodded numbly.

And just like that, it was done.

In a few short minutes, Abe produced contracts with stipulations and non-disclosure agreements, all of which Lily read through at Abe's desk while her grandmother napped on the loveseat, clutching her precious flip-phone cord and snoring softly. Jud sat in a chair on the other side of the room, reading his papers.

They finished signing at about the same time.

The clock ticked like a timer on a bomb. For surely, this

was going to blow up in Lily's face, like that time she'd taken Dad's Ferrari for a joy ride in the Hamptons and gotten pulled over in front of the trendiest restaurant that summer. She'd been fifteen and thought rules hadn't applied to her, just like her dear friend Rachel, who got whatever she wanted regardless of the consequences. But unlike Rachel, Lily had grown up. And she had Rachel to thank for that.

Speaking of wanting...

Lily's gaze drifted to Jud. He could have any woman he wanted. "Why did you kiss me?"

Jud capped his pen, set it down, and straightened his contract. "You know...Rachel is...There's no easy way to say this. Rachel is a nice person. But she has a wandering eye and is free with her hands. When I told Abe we were a couple, it was because I thought he wanted me to sing at her wedding. I panicked. I wanted a defense."

"And I was convenient." Lily's insides squeezed hard enough to squash what little confidence she had left. "Rachel's engaged. You won't need a buffer or a defense."

Jud tsked, wagging his finger at her. "Don't forget Rachel married someone else a little over two months ago. If you haven't seen her lately, what Abe says is true. She can be... irrational when it comes to logic. And she's a bit paranoid, as if everyone is out to get her."

Great. "If this is your version of a pep talk..."

"If you're looking for an excuse not to go..." Jud shrugged, studying Lily's face. "From what Abe said, I take it you and Rachel had a falling out."

"Growing up, Rachel, my sister Violet, and I used to be good friends." It was Lily's turn to cap her pen, set it down, and tidy her contract sheets. "And then when we were seventeen, Rachel's mother died, and she fell apart." Not even Lily's good intentions could put her together again.

"Did she steal your boyfriend?" Jud asked straight-faced. "That seems to be her modus operandi."

"If only it were that simple."

Jud's eyes widened. "What did Rachel do? You can tell me. I've already agreed to keep all the Cohen secrets. I may as well pinky swear to keep all yours." His smile was magnetic, as disarming in real life as on the screen.

Lily wanted to smile, wanted to melt, but...

They may have teamed up on this task to save Rachel from herself but giving in to temptation with a hunky actor would only complicate things down the road. "I'd rather not say."

"Come on, Lily. It helps to talk about it," Jud said softly. His tone of voice reached something deep inside of Lily and grabbed hold, as if instinctively she knew they could be something to each other. "This is like the teaser my show does before a commercial break to ensure the audience hangs around to see what happens next to Titanium Talon." The superhero character he played on TV.

"I'll tell you what happened." Grandma Dotty sat up and yawned. "After her mama died, Rachel got upset when Abe tried to rein her in. She ran away from home. Only she wasn't brave enough to run away alone, so she took Lily with her. We were lucky Lily returned home unscathed."

Unscathed? Lily forced herself to breath steadily–four counts in, four counts out.

Jud's gaze turned compassionate.

Lily didn't want his compassion or his pity. "Let's just say that was the straw that ended our friendship." After that, Lily's adventures had been tests of her courage and limited to forays with Violet glued to her side.

Grandma Dotty harumphed. "Because of Rachel–"

"I'd rather not relive the past." Lily kept it locked up in a box in her memory attic.

"And yet, you're going to face it head on," Jud pointed out.

A surge of uncertainty had Lily staring at the papers she'd signed and considering tearing them up.

"So, Lily, you either agreed to Abe's intervention plan because you feel responsible for Rachel's life derailing or..." Jud stood and helped Grandma Dotty to her feet. "...because you still hold a grudge over what happened."

"I'm not responsible for who she is today." Lily frowned, searching her motivations. "Beyond the donation... I signed because Rachel could use a friend. Abe said none of hers support this marriage."

Jud shrugged. "We all tell ourselves the truth we want to believe."

Suddenly, Lily wasn't sure what to think about herself, Rachel, or the past. "Gosh, look at the time. I need to text Ryan that we're ready to head home." She bent her head over her phone.

"I need to use the facilities before we go." Grandma Dotty yawned again as she made her exit, leaving Lily and Jud alone.

Text complete, Lily's gaze went to Jud's mouth. The excitement of being in his arms rushed back, as intense as that feeling of cresting a rollercoaster's first big hill, one that dropped quickly down the other side. She squeezed her eyes shut. "I don't suppose you can get your own ride."

"You wouldn't ditch your boyfriend in the middle of the night, would you?" Those words. So layered with invitation, innuendo, and tease.

Lily's eyes flew open. "*Fake* boyfriend."

That smile of his...How could she love it and hate it at the same time?

"Even fake boyfriends have benefits."

Lily took a step back. "Car rides and hand holding. That's it."

"More like long slow kisses in front of an audience." Jud's gaze descended upon her lips.

Lily gasped, darting out of the library and toward the front door. "Our relationship is only just developing, remember? And we're not sharing a room onboard."

"Aren't we?" Jud captured Lily's hand, slowing her down enough to give her a mischievous smile. "Admit it. You liked it when I kissed you."

Her pulse pounded out an answer she didn't like. His kisses were hot and she wanted another.

"There will be no more kissing." She should have paperwork for that–the No Kissing Contract. "We have a job to do."

"You never heard of mixing business with pleasure?" Judson put a hand on the front door, keeping Lily from bolting for the elevator and leaving Grandma Dotty behind. "That's a shame. That's a real shame."

3

———————

"The network needs an answer Friday, Jud." Darian Rutledge, Jud's agent, stood next to him at the entrance to the slip where Abe's yacht was docked. "The money they're offering for three more seasons of Titanium Talon is enough to fund your little indie film later."

"Don't jump the gun. I told you that Abe Cohen is going to put up five million." The ocean swells rocked the dock beneath Jud's feet and challenged his equilibrium. The brisk ocean breeze ruffled Jud's hair. But he refused to let his agent's negativity ruffle his resolve. "That leaves me with another fifteen million to raise." Either through a loan or investors. "Ten if I put up five."

Jud wished he felt better about the job that was required to earn Abe's five-million-dollar investment. Stopping Rachel's wedding gave a whole new meaning to the term cut-throat. Not even Lily's sweet kisses could absolve him of that sin if the couple were truly in love.

"You're giving up millions–*guaranteed money*–to make a movie that could sink your career?" Darian was beside himself, looking out of place on the dock in his blue Tom Ford suit and red power tie. "Listen to what you're saying."

"Darian, I'm grateful for everything you've done for me, but you know I've been searching for a new challenge." Jud wasn't absolutely certain that directing was what he was looking for, but it was what actors did when they felt creatively burnt out. "The network loves to see me featured with my latest date in the gossip magazines. It brings in viewers. If I sign that contract, that's what they'll expect of me—titillating gossip about the latest celebrity I'm dating. There's more to me than that." He had his eye on the long-term game. "It's why I want to date someone different. Someone less...titillating. Someone who the gossip rags find boring and who doesn't tempt me. Honestly, I just want a fake date. And I found the perfect woman for the role."

"You want to give up mega-acting deals and date Mary Poppins?" Darian glanced away, frowning.

Why? Because he didn't want to reduce Jud's exposure in the tabloids? Or because... "You don't think I have what it takes to direct." Jud didn't phrase it as a question. He didn't bother to disguise his hurt, either. "Need I remind you that I'm a Hambly? Or that my family has a case filled with ten Oscars?" Directing was in his blood. He'd practically been raised on movie sets. "I can do this."

Not to mention his family expected him to. When his father had won the Oscar for his directorial debut, he'd laid down the gauntlet to Jud, saying, *"God willing, my son's going to carry on the family tradition and win this for directing one day."*

"Direct a short or a documentary first, not a feature." The wind blew Darian's red tie into the air. It flailed about until Darian caught it. "If I represented your father at your age, I would have given him the same advice."

Jud wasn't buying it. He saw greed in Darian's eyes, not sincerity.

"Darian..." Jud wasn't sure what to say. He glanced at the large yacht towering beside them. It had sleek lines but the tackiest light sconces along the exterior deck–a tangle of black metal strips with glass peeking out.

"Ah, here he is." Darian pointed to a man with a camera on the other side of the security fence who aimed a football-sized lens their way.

Click-click-click.

Darian's expression returned to the pleasant smile that was his baseline. "Before you take up with a boring fake girl-friend, maybe my friend with the camera can capture a shot of you with Rachel Cohen. She's got plenty of buzz around her." Jud's agent wasn't giving up on the status quo.

"*Yoohoo!*" a woman's warbly voice called.

"No need to decide about the network offer today, Jud. You're going on a private cruise." Darian tucked his tie back beneath his jacket. "You're flying back on Friday. I'll tell the network to expect your answer then."

"*Yoohoo!* Yes, I'm talking to you." Dotty mashed a floppy straw hat on her head, shouldered a large red tapestry bag, and wheeled a small black suitcase behind her. She wove her way down the ramp like a race car navigating the curves on Mulholland Drive. "A little help, oh, hero mine."

Jud hurried to assist the old woman before she fell into the harbor. "Dotty, what are you doing here?" She wasn't supposed to be sailing with them. "Does Lily know you're coming?"

"Of course not. But I'm an adult with bank accounts and charge cards of my own." Dotty wore a pink velour track suit, white orthopedic sneakers, and pearls. She put her floppy hat on Jud's head, which elicited several camera clicks. "Not to mention Abe invited me, too. I gave up a vow of silence for this trip and I'm going to enjoy talking and singing during every minute of it."

"You know this woman?" Darian frowned.

"Of course, Jud knows me. We spent *hours* together last night." Dotty's short white hair blew this way and that in the breeze. Uncaring, she turned her attention to Jud. "Did you bring your superhero suit? I'd like to try it on."

Oh. Jud wasn't sure what to say to that.

Darian knew what to say. "No superhero suit for you, ma'am." He swiped Dotty's hat from Jud's head just as the porter who'd collected Jud's luggage hurried down the yacht's gang plank. He handed the straw hat to the porter, directing him to take Dotty's bags from Jud. "I'm sure you brought your knitting to keep you busy."

"Knitting?" Dotty snorted. "What kind of grandma do you think I am, young man? I brought my two-piece. I anticipate singing show tunes in the hot tub every night with Jud." Head held high, Dotty followed the porter up the gang plank belting out *Seventy Six Trombones.*

Jud grinned. Props to the old gal for handling a high-powered talent agent as if he were a middle schooler.

"I thought you were cruising with Rachel Cohen?" Darian scrubbed a hand over his short black hair. "A picture with you and Grandma is worth nothing to our network deal."

"Forget the network deal," Jud said through gritted teeth.

"Shoot." Lily came down the ramp toting a much larger suitcase than her grandmother had packed. Hair in a loose bun, she wore blue Keds, blue jeans, a soft blue crew neck sweater. Her black frames had slid down on her nose. "Tell me that wasn't my grandmother getting on board just now."

Jud rushed forward to greet Lily with a quick hug and a

kiss to her cheek, which was not enthusiastically received. "I'm not going to tell you anything that might upset you, honey. Look." He slung his arm over Lily's shoulders and pointed to the cameraman.

Lily smoothly slipped from beneath his embrace, but not fast enough to escape the paparazzi. "Is that the wedding photographer?"

"I don't think so." Jud collected her suitcase handle and wheeled it to the gang plank. "Let's call it practice." He introduced her to Darian. "Lily is my date this week. You just met her grandmother."

Darian's mouth dropped open. "But she's…"

"*My date.*" Jud gave Lily a smile designed to charm, which wasn't hard considering he found her charming.

"Oh. *That* date," Darian said knowingly, earning Lily's raised brows.

The porter returned for Lily's suitcase.

"Please tell me I'm sharing a room with my grandmother," Lily said, eyes firmly on the porter. "She's in need of a keeper."

"Yes, ma'am." The porter led the way up the gang plank.

"*Ma'am,*" Lily muttered, shaking her head as she followed him.

"I have no idea what you're doing," Darian said once Lily had reached the yacht. "But I can tell it's not in your best interest. I'll pay the photographer to delete the photos with Mary Poppins and Grandma. But I beg you. Don't get on that ship."

"I know what I'm doing," Jud said in a tone meant to end the discussion. "In order to garner financing, I need a girlfriend who is safe and mundane. There's no one safer or more mundane than Lily Summer."

"All right, but just remember that you're going against

my recommendation." Darian had a hand over his heart, most likely to keep his tie in place, but it made his statement seem oddly sincere. "Be careful. I'll pick you up Friday and expect an answer for the network."

Jud lingered at the slip entrance long after Darian had left, thinking about the paths ahead of him. It was hard enough to make it in Hollywood as an actor, much less branch out into writing, directing or producing. Darian had guided Jud's career from his teenage years through today. For that, Jud would be forever grateful. But it was increasingly clear that he and Darian weren't on the same page. Or perhaps it was Jud's father and uncle, the ones pushing him to direct, who weren't on the same page as Jud. He felt torn.

A black stretch limo pulled up to the ramp.

Abe Cohen got out, dressed in khakis and a gray polo shirt. The wind flattened his spiked hair. He helped his daughter Rachel out of the far side of the car. The wind tossed her long red hair about before she caught it with one hand. Nearest to Jud, a very tall man unfurled himself, stretching his arms like an eagle about to take flight. His head was clean-shaven, and he wore a green silk button-down shirt over blue jeans and fancy sneakers.

The photographer snapped away at the new arrivals as they made their way to the ramp.

"Judson Hambly, my very own silver-tongued devil." Rachel wore a teal bodycon dress and matching heels that weren't made for seafaring. She strutted her way down the ramp without waiting for her father or her fiancé.

Jud knew women. From the way Rachel was taking him in, he was picking up vibes and they weren't of the platonic variety. It was good for his mission here and yet the entire fiber of his being went on red alert.

Where was Lily? He needed her.

Rachel came to a halt in front of Jud and doled out air kisses that came with a suggestive whisper of hot air over each ear. "I'm so glad you agreed to be Paulo's best man." She ran her hands over Jud's shoulders, squeezing his biceps the way a savvy shopper squeezed avocados at the market before buying.

Click-click-click went the photographer.

"Best man?" Jud managed to choke out. The Cohens really were scraping the bottom of the barrel for attendees. It was his turn to speak, but his instincts were urging him to flee.

Lily appeared next to Jud, looping her arm through his and drawing him a safe distance away from the touchy-feely bride. "I thought I saw you drive up, Rachel. Congratulations on your engagement. And thank you for the wedding invitation. *We're* honored to attend." Lily said all the right things at all the right times.

"Lily Summer." Rachel did a catty woman's once-over of Lily, gaze lingering too long on her arm linked through Jud's. "I saw you at the charity event last night. In fact, I saw both of you...Just not together."

"We'd hoped to keep our relationship quiet a little bit longer." Jud placed his hand over Lily's cold one, grateful that she'd come to his rescue, wondering if a kiss was in order.

A kiss with Lily should always be in order.

That was nerves talking...wasn't it?

The groom approached them with ground-eating strides. "I'm Paulo." And then he smiled and said something in a foreign language.

Rachel tittered. "Isn't he sweetness?"

"He is." Lily agreed. She rattled off some words in a similar dialect, blushing slightly as she caught Jud's eye. "I know enough Spanish to get by. I think Paulo's speaking Portuguese. He says it's lovely to meet so many good friends. He said Judson is a good man...an unusual man...no." Lily beamed. "The *best* man." And then she glanced at Jud with a question in her eyes.

"That's me." Best man for sale. A bargain at five million dollars.

Paulo rattled off another sentence or two, grinning at Lily.

"With so many good friends, it bodes well for my marriage, he says." Lily continued to translate. She glanced at Rachel. "Do you speak Portuguese?"

Rachel shook her head, sidling next to Paulo. "We've always had our own special language."

"The language of love?" Jud guessed, suppressing the urge to grin.

Rachel nodded. "We should get on board. We'll have drinks in the main lounge as we embark, and my wedding planner will review our itinerary." She sashayed up the gang plank on Paulo's arm. "We dress up for dinner, Lily. I hope you packed accordingly."

"Thanks for the rescue," Jud whispered in Lily's ear.

"I saw their limo arrive from the deck. I figured you might need an assist." Lily shaded her eyes, watching the bride and groom ascend to the yacht. "From the way Rachel looked at me, I'll need a rescue of my own. But from the way she looked at you..." Lily gave him a speculative look. "I think I know how to stop the wedding."

"I don't like that conniving look in your eyes." It made him want to kiss her until a dreamier expression lit up her face.

"Conniving?" Lily stiffened. "We're helping to get her back on track. It's just... Tell me you lost sleep last night over this deal. Tell me..."

"You're having second thoughts about stopping the wedding," Jud guessed.

She nodded.

"Me, too." He drew her back toward the ramp leading up to the parking lot. "Let's make a pact. If Rachel and Paulo truly love each other, we won't try to sabotage their special day."

"Agreed." Lily hugged him, pulling back almost immediately, blushing profusely, perhaps because the photographer's camera was clicking like mad. She adjusted her glasses. "That said, I think we should–"

"All aboard." Abe tucked his wallet in his back pocket as he came down the ramp to the boat slip. "We depart as soon as the wedding planner arrives and our luggage is stowed away."

"We'll talk later," Jud promised.

Lily dutifully headed up the gang plank.

Jud caught Abe's arm, briefly halting his progress. "Where are the other wedding guests?" According to the porter, Jud had been the first to arrive.

"There are no other guests." Abe clapped a hand on Jud's shoulder before stepping onto the gang plank.

The weight of his words sank in. "It's just us?"

Lily paused, turning halfway up the gang plank. "But...if Jud is the best man, that means I'm...the maid of honor?"

"You catch on quick." Abe walked past her.

Lily stared into Jud's eyes before glancing toward the ramp, the harbor building, and the New York skyline. "Every time I think this trip is challenging my moral bar, it just sinks lower. The best man and maid of honor are supposed to do everything to make a wedding day go off without a hitch."

And instead, they'd be doing just the opposite.

"You can't bail. Not yet." Jud walked quickly toward her, thinking of all that was at stake–a film, his credibility in the industry, his family's approval. "Your grandmother is already on board. Maybe we'll get lucky and not only will we recognize they're in love, but Abe will, too. No matter what happens, we'll get through this." He grabbed Lily's hand and led her up the plank. "Together."

"With our moral compasses intact?"

He didn't answer. But he hoped so.

"You shouldn't have come," Lily told Grandma Dotty as she unpacked in their small stateroom, wrestling with her conscience and concerns about Rachel's dismissive attitude toward her. Of all the ways she'd imagined their reunion going, this hot and cold reception wasn't it. "I get the impression that Rachel is considering whether it's open season on Lily Summer or not." And if Lily stopped her wedding, she'd have every right to retaliate.

"You've seen her show. She's changed a little since you were kids. Rachel is out to get everyone before they get her. All the more reason to have your granny in your corner." Dotty lay on her back on her single bed and raised her legs up in the air, and then lowered them over her head. "That's why I'm stretching. I don't want to pull something if there's going to be a brawl."

"There won't be a brawl." Just five days of floating through rough waters. "I can take whatever Rachel throws at me because her father is going to feed and shelter those in need in my district."

"Saint Lily, eh?" Dotty returned her legs to the recline position. "You were never a saint."

Lily nearly dropped her cocktail dress. "That's a horrible thing to say."

"I don't see why." Dotty sat up, smoothing the short white hair she'd slicked back upon arrival. "No one in the Summer clan is an angel, including me."

"You're a saint," Lily insisted. "And so am I."

"Pfft." Dotty got to her feet and took the two short steps to reach Lily's side. "Saints are angels who've died and gone to heaven." She tugged the pins from Lily's hair. "You need to let your hair down or when you're my age, you'll have a bucket list longer than your arm."

"Don't." But it was too late. Grandma Dotty had removed all Lily's pins. Her hair came down to rest below her shoulders.

"Now you look like you belong on this fancy floating hotel." Grandma Dotty stepped back to admire her work, frowning. "Or you would if you'd change into something snazzier. What I could have done if I'd had those legs of yours."

"I'm not changing. It's spring and we're sailing on the Atlantic Ocean. It's going to be cold." Lily tugged on Grandma Dotty's pink velour jacket sleeve. "You're dressed for warmth."

"You should dress to keep Jud's eyes on you, not Rachel. I saw that girl through the peephole. She only had eyes for your man."

"He's not mine. And I'm assuming you mean the *port*hole." Which you could only look out if you stood on one of the beds.

"Peephole. Porthole." Grandma Dotty shrugged. "You knew what I meant."

"Yes. But I don't mind if Rachel is interested in Jud." That felt like a lie, as unsettling as her mission to talk Rachel out of getting married.

This isn't me.

Grandma Dotty seemed to agree. Her brow was puckered as if she was confused by Lily's words.

There was a knock on the door.

"Ladies." Not only did Jud look handsome as sin in his khakis and black polo shirt, he looked pleased to see them. "Can I escort you to the lounge and the embarking party?"

Grandma Dotty took three steps to the door and opened it. "Only if they're serving sandwiches, preferably egg salad."

"I'm sure whatever they're serving is wonderful." The last thing Lily wanted was to be difficult.

"Shrimp cocktail, I'm betting." Grandma Dotty shrugged. "Shrimp gives me the toots."

"I'll risk it." Lily adjusted her glasses, avoiding meeting Jud's gaze lest she succumb to a smile. "I just need a few more minutes to unpack."

"Take your time." Her grandmother nodded her head slowly as she considered Jud. "While you finish, I'll check out Jud's room. If it's larger than ours, I'm not giving this trip a good review." She sashayed out the door.

"I don't think Abe has a review page, Dotty," Jud said, blue eyes twinkling. He shut the door behind them.

Their footsteps receded. Their voices grew faint. Lily was left alone with a mindless task and too much weighing on her mind. The pit in her stomach said she was crossing a line, no matter how many times her head argued it was worth stopping a rushed wedding to feed and shelter so many people and to help Rachel see her way to making better choices. And if it turned out Rachel and Paulo were madly in love? Well, Lily hoped Abe would support Hot Meals and Shelter anyway.

The cabin door burst open just as Lily hung up her last blouse.

Grandma Dotty barged in. "Jud's room is bigger than ours–bigger bed, bigger closet, and he has a soaker tub. And to answer your unspoken question–I checked, and no, he didn't bring his supersuit."

"That depends on your definition of supersuit." Jud's sultry glance gave his words layers of meaning.

Oh, my.

Lily's doubts sailed away. And they'd keep sailing if Jud continued to drop those flirty lines.

Grandma Dotty was stuck on Jud's hero gear. "Young man, my definition of a supersuit is gunmetal gray tights and that black body armor of yours. How could you leave it at home? What if they send up the Titanium Talon signal while we're on this cruise?" Grandma Dotty tsked, as if Jud might neglect his superhero duties. "I suppose in a pinch, I'll let Jud borrow my support hose and you can let him wear your one piece, Lily. It's black, isn't it?"

Jud's mouth dropped open.

"Now, come on. Let's go. I'm famished." Grandma Dotty marched out the door and toward the oval staircase that rose four stories through the center of the yacht.

Lily felt obligated to clarify things. "Grandma Dotty, you're confusing Jud with the role he plays on TV."

"I'm not." Grandma Dotty waved a hand above her head. "Jud arrived with a sidekick. I think it's you who's confused."

Uh-oh. Was Grandma Dotty losing touch with reality?

"Look at me." Lily caught her grandmother's arm and turned her until they were facing each other. She stared deep into her grandmother's faded, slightly unfocused eyes. "Count backward from one hundred."

Worry flashed across her grandmother's features. She opened her mouth and then closed it again.

"Grandma Dotty..."

Her grandmother reached up to place her cool palms on Lily's cheeks. "I'm still here. I'm not going to count backward to prove it."

"Okay, but you were talking as if superheroes were real."

"Superheroes *are* real," Grandma Dotty insisted. "I married one. And if you're lucky, you'll snag one, too." She gave Jud a significant look. "Don't settle for a sidekick. Aim high."

The boat shuddered as the engines started up, and then quieted as the motors settled into a low rumble.

Lily's cell phone chimed with a text message. She gave it a quick read before climbing the stairs, growing more agitated with each step. "You didn't tell Dad you were leaving? He's asking where I am and if you're with me." She'd ignored his calls and texts all morning. And she hadn't answered the door when he'd knocked. Her father could be exhausting, and Lily was already exhausted.

"Running away from home is on my bucket list." Grandma Dotty tsked. "Check that one off."

Lily tapped out a quick message. "I just texted him that we're both fine."

"Drat. You know what happens when you answer his messages..." Grandma Dotty clapped her hands at least ten times. "*Call-mageddon*. Your father refuses to acknowledge personal boundaries unless they're his own. I turned off my flip phone. Follow my lead and turn off your cell phone."

"But..."

Jud gently plucked Lily's phone from her hand. "I'm with Dotty on this one." He turned it off and handed it back to Lily. "We have enough to worry about and he knows you're both fine."

There was that, she supposed.

They reached the second level of the yacht, which had a bar with a bartender, and a swanky lounge with white chairs and couches on whitewashed wood floors. It opened to a viewing deck over the rear of the boat.

Rachel sat on a couch with her feet curled up, leaning into Paulo. They both held champagne flutes. They looked content.

But were they in love?

"Champagne?" the bartender asked.

"Not for my grandmother," Lily said firmly as she took a glass of champagne from the bartender. "No drinks the entire trip. It interferes with her meds."

"Fine." Grandma Dotty harumphed. "I promise not to drink, but I don't promise not to dance or sing. Now, first things first. I'd like an egg salad sandwich." She nodded toward the bartender, who picked up a phone and relayed her order, presumably to the kitchen.

The yacht slowly pulled away from its moorings.

"We talked about sidekicks earlier?" Dotty's brow furrowed as she focused on Jud. "But that man in the suit on the dock isn't your sidekick."

"No. Darian is my agent."

"You could do better," Grandma Dotty said crisply, turning her back on a tray of shrimp cocktail. "Like that kickbutt sidekick of Titanium Talon's. That woman. She wears an owl costume."

"It's actually meant to look like a world war two fighter

pilot uniform," Jud explained. "That's why she's called Aviator."

"That's right." Dotty snapped her fingers. "Aviator. But I don't get the uniform impression. Her lady bubbles are ringed to look like owl eyes."

Lily choked on her champagne, agreeing with her grandmother but that didn't mean she wanted boobage to be the topic of discussion with men present.

"That's...not...right." Jud frowned. "Her costume is a nod to the men who served in World War Two."

"That's a stretch," Lily felt the need to stick up for Grandma Dotty regardless of it not being an appropriate subject for a social gathering. "Her costume is brown with darker armor around her..."

"Snuggle pups," Grandma Dotty finished for Lily, moving toward a fruit bowl.

"Man lures," Rachel contributed from the couch, placing a hand beneath her abundant assets for emphasis and smiling, reminding Lily of her sense of humor. Maybe the time Lily had spent worrying about how Rachel would react to her presence had all been for naught. "I agree. She looks like an owl."

"Aviator is *not* a bird," Jud insisted.

"Then explain the dark circles around her Lily-hammers." Grandma Dotty held up two apples.

"It does seem sexist, like they want men to notice her Big Kahunas." Rachel grinned.

"When she runs, you might call them bouncy castles." Lily couldn't resist playing along.

"Flabbergasters." Grandma Dotty giggled.

"Cha-cha bingos." Rachel chortled, nearly spilling her drink. "Before I had breast reduction surgery, I heard them all." Her expression sobered.

"I always hated the way people judged you by your bra size," Lily said softly, earning a grateful smile from Rachel, who may have reduced her cha-cha bingos, but still had no trouble filling out a bra.

"All right. All right. Enough." Jud ordered a whiskey from the bartender. "If I sign on to play Titanium Talon another three seasons, I'll ask for some costume changes."

"Ask them to enlarge your cod piece while you're at it." Dotty went to sit next to Paulo.

"*I* don't need a larger anything." Jud glared at them all.

Paulo raised his fist and said something that Lily translated to mean, *"Work with God's gifts, no matter how small."*

"What did he say?" Jud sipped his drink.

"He's a fan," Lily lied. She finished her champagne in one big gulp.

A middle-aged woman joined them. She had a pixie-cut, dyed hot pink, wore a brown pantsuit and an air of importance. "I'm Marta, the wedding coordinator." She proceeded to go over their schedule. "We have wardrobe fittings and hairstyling this afternoon. We hope to dock in Norfolk tonight, which will allow jet skiing in the morning for anyone who wants to explore the bay."

"Jet skiing. That's on my bucket list," Grandma Dotty chimed in, grinning from ear-to-ear. "Who's gonna race me?"

"Challenge accepted." Jud walked over and gave her a high five. And then he came to stand next to Lily in the middle of the room.

"She has to ride double with someone," Lily said, feeling like the trip's spoilsport.

"You can be my wingman, Lily." Grandma Dotty didn't miss a beat.

"Anyway..." Marta gave Lily a sideways look before

continuing. "We'll dock in Charleston tomorrow night and spend the morning taking care of wedding fixes I can't handle." She took in Lily's appearance, reaching out to touch Lily's hair. "Worst case, we call in a professional stylist when we get to Miami Beach."

Lily contained an eye-roll. "My hair is long enough for an updo."

"We'll see," Marta said in a dour voice.

"Makeovers. That sounds like fun. Can I be a bridesmaid, too?" Dotty aimed her genial smile at Rachel.

"Of course," Rachel said with a laugh. "You can never have too many bridesmaids."

"Hot dog!" Dotty turned that smile toward Lily. "Being a bridesmaid again is on my bucket list."

"Is there anything not on her bucket list?" Jud murmured in a voice only Lily could hear.

"Nope." With a wry smile, Lily raised her glass. "Here's to bucket lists and sacrifices made for the greater good."

Jud, Rachel, and Paulo raised their glasses.

Marta wasn't interested in toasts. "We don't have to be in Miami Beach until Thursday night, which allows us the option of either staying two nights in Charleston or stopping in another Florida port."

"I prefer a flexible schedule." Rachel ran a hand over Paulo's chest, but her gaze was stuck on Jud.

Which upset Lily on too many levels, some of them in opposition to each other: *Don't look at Jud like that!* And: *Yes, choose Jud over Paulo and cancel the wedding!*

A crew member hurried up the stairs carrying a plate with a sandwich. He was the same young man who'd helped with their luggage. "Your egg salad, ma'am."

"Thank you." Grandma Dotty accepted the plate and then glanced down at it. "Why is it so brown?"

"Chef made it with curry and fried apple shreds," the young man explained.

"I'm a woman of simple tastes." Grandma Dotty handed the plate back. "Tell the chef to try again."

4

Rachel stared at Jud like a dieter who'd been served a hot fudge sundae with a warm spoon.

Jud should have welcomed that look, encouraged that look, emboldened her to do more than look. That look could earn him an investor.

Not like this.

"Lily, will you look at that view," Jud said instead, gesturing toward the receding New York City skyline, sparkling in the morning sun. "Come on, honey." Jud led Lily away from Rachel and out to the viewing deck where they leaned on the rail. The same homely black metal exterior lights that were illuminating the side decks were out here. In fact, they were all over the public areas of the yacht, making him wonder if Rachel had partnered with the maker and intended to mass produce them.

Coming soon to a home improvement box store near you.

"Sorry about my grandmother. And the Aviator. And the way Rachel won't stop looking at you." Lily stared at her hands. "The amount of regrets I'm having doesn't bode well for this trip."

"Let's not talk regrets before we determine the depth of Rachel's feelings for Paulo." The groom seemed smitten with Rachel, but Rachel was still transmitting signals that argued against her being in love. Jud inched closer to Lily, partly because Rachel would notice he was taken, and partly because he liked being close to Lily. "Are you cold? I could put my arm around you." He hoped she'd say yes.

"In for a penny..." Lily gave him a resigned smile. "Go for it, Talon."

"Talon *would* go for it." Jud limited his moves to an arm over Lily's shoulders. But he drew her close. "I know it's torture to be in my arms."

"Like your kisses." She rolled her eyes. "A test of my endurance."

Now that was taking things a little too far.

Stung, Jud drew Lily closer still, whispering in her ear, "I've had few complaints about my kissing technique." Much less hear women refer to his kisses as requiring endurance.

"It's not that, I...I wouldn't complain if we knew each other better." Lily blushed. "Not that I'm asking you to make it real. It's like... It's like going to the store and eating the food samples they're handing out for lunch when you know you aren't going to buy the family-sized pack of frozen pizza rolls they're selling."

"I'm the frozen pizza rolls in this metaphor?" His pride was getting a good trampling today.

Lily stared at the water churning beneath them. "You didn't feel awkward kissing me last night? We're strangers."

"I don't want to sound like a man-whore, but as a TV commercial actor in my teens, I showed up on the set and kissed a girl on camera within an hour of meeting her."

Her brows lowered in disapproval. "*Acting.*"

Jud ran a thumb across the wrinkle in her brow, smoothing it away. "Our kiss may have started as a ruse, but it was sincerely felt."

She smirked.

She didn't believe him? "I have a genuine need to kiss you again." *That's right, girl.* He arched his brows. Need, not want. "No acting required. Now, share your evil plan to stop the wedding."

Lily leaned on her elbow, half turning to face him without moving from beneath his arm. "It's simple, not evil," she whispered. "I know I can't *talk* Rachel out of anything. So, today and tomorrow, we act like a happy couple. Then on Wednesday, we stage a big fight. Rachel will want to comfort you. And you'll make your move. If she doesn't love Paulo, the wedding will be canceled."

No.

Jud took a beat. His gut reaction was surprising and it came from... He stared into Lily's big brown eyes behind those glasses. Her gaze was straightforward, the same as her plan. That was the thing about Lily, he realized. She didn't come to him with hidden agendas. His gut reaction came more from not wanting to break up with mundane Lily than offering himself up as the sacrificial lamb with the hungry-eyed Rachel.

"But..." Like clockwork, uncertainty crept into Lily's gaze. "What if they love each other?"

Jud drew a deep breath. "Then I'll find another way to finance my dream and you'll find another way to feed the hungry and provide refuge to folks who need it." He drew her into the shelter of both his arms, drawing comfort and hoping he gave some in return. "How can you tell if some-one's in love?"

"I don't know. I have a three date limit." Her arms came

around his waist. Her lips moved closer to his ear as she began to whisper, "Is it when that person brings out the best in you?"

"I always thought it had to do with a level of trust and deep understanding." Jud's hands roamed slowly across her back. "That's how all the great script writers I've worked with have put it into words."

"Trust comes hard for me," Lily admitted in a voice filled with regret.

"A result of that adventure Rachel convinced you to go on?"

Lily didn't deny it. "All those women you've dated... You've never been in love?" Lily drew back slightly, staring up at his face.

Jud shook his head and then brushed a lock of wind-blown brown hair away from her eyes. "If I had, I'd know what love is." *It would feel like this.*

"Same, I guess." Lily put her head on his shoulder. "My career makes it hard to meet someone outside politics. I'm not one for nightlife." She gently plucked at his shirt sleeve. "I bet that sounds boring to you."

"You say that like you think I'm out on the town every night."

Lily shrugged. "Whether you are or you aren't, it's none of my business. All I'm saying is I've become as predictable as the New Year's Eve ball dropping on Times Square, whereas you..."

"Hang on. Aren't you the woman taking late night meetings and impromptu yacht vacations?"

Lily gave a little laugh. "I am, aren't I?" Her words rang with pride.

"What's this?" Dotty piped up in the lounge. The old woman didn't bother accepting the plate the crew member brought her this time. She peered at it suspiciously. "I asked for an egg salad sandwich."

The young man holding the sandwich grimaced. "The chef thought you'd enjoy egg salad and anchovies with pickled peppers."

Dotty tossed her hands. "Egg salad. That's all I want. Send it back."

Next to her, Marta clapped her hands. "Attention. It's time for the bon voyage pictures. Everyone move to the rail." She had a serious-looking camera hanging around her neck.

Paulo helped Rachel and Dotty to their feet. The trio joined Jud and Lily at the railing. There was a group photo and then several photos of Rachel and Paulo. Abe was a no show.

"They look like they adore each other," Lily whispered to Jud.

He stared down at Lily, feeling like he could adore her.

What?

Jud reminded himself of the demands of his career and his plans for Lily to be a convenient date when needed.

But he couldn't quite shake the sense that Lily was over-qualified for the role.

Let the bridesmaid duties begin!

Lily entered the salon below decks after lunch, expecting to be inundated with engine noise. But when Marta closed the door behind them, it was blessedly quiet.

The salon was more like a beauty spa. There was a hair stylist chair, a massage table, and a pedicure lounger. The walls were covered with seagrass wallpaper. The floor with bamboo planks. The room was lit with heavy, black metal wall sconces that were everywhere throughout the yacht but at odds with the otherwise light, luxurious décor.

The juxtaposition was just as odd as how uncivilly Rachel had greeted Lily on the dock and then seemed more amenable to her presence during the yacht's leaving port. Jud had warned Lily about Rachel's mercurial nature. It kept her on pins and needles. She wasn't going to be relaxing in this spa.

"Ladies, you have three choices in bridesmaid dresses." Wasting no time, Marta brought three dresses from a closet. Her pink hair glowed nearly neon in the light.

"I didn't want to force my style on my attendants." Rachel sat in a pedicure lounger, turning on the tap and tossing in some bath salts. Unlike Lily's tangled locks, her red hair was wind-tossed but attractively so. "Ladies choice. You don't even have to match."

Immediately, Grandma Dotty began inspecting their options, while Lily peeked into the closet. It was filled with clothing of all styles and colors. "What are these for?"

"My mood," Rachel said simply. But her gaze was anything but simple. In fact, it seemed layered with dangerous undercurrents.

And here we go.

Lily braced herself for whatever attack Rachel decided to launch, wishing Jud were at her side. It was cowardly, but Lily imagined she could withstand whatever Rachel said to her if she and Jud were together.

"I'll be darned." Grandma Dotty held a cream and silver dress up to her shoulders. "This is a two-piece."

"The top is a simple V-neck cream chiffon." Marta went into bridal consultant mode. "The silver skirt is floor-length, A-line. And it has pockets."

"Pockets," Grandma Dotty breathed in apparent wonder.

"As simple as a plain egg salad sandwich. What they won't think of next. Do you like it, Lily?"

Lily nodded. It was casual and feminine. It would be comfortable in any uncomfortable situation.

"We also have a black strapless gown with a beaded bodice." Marta held up the second option. "It has a beautiful, floor-length skirt."

"And a slit up to my hoo-ha." Holding the dress to her shoulders, Grandma Dotty extended one pink track-suited leg forward and struck a pose. "I'm no Angelina Jolie. Does it come with matching panties?"

Marta pressed her lips together and shook her head, although her action didn't disturb a single pink hair.

"Pass?" Lily asked her grandmother.

"Pass." Grandma Dotty took the dress from Marta and returned it to the closet. "What else do you have?"

Marta radiated displeasure from the tight line of her mouth to her narrowed eyes. "The third option is a burgundy asymmetrical gown with cap sleeves. The skirt hits just below the knees in front and is full length on the back and sides. This gown won't fall off or trip you unless you walk backward." Marta held out the skirt for Grandma Dotty's inspection. "It plunges in the back. Very sexy."

"No pockets though." Lily's grandmother snatched that away as well. "We'll take the two-piece, please."

"I always try a dress on before making a final decision." Rachel settled back into the pedicure lounger. "You never know what works for you until you try. That's also been my philosophy with men, although my dad hates that I think that way."

"But if it works for you…" Lily handed her grandmother the strapless gown. Might just as well start with the least likely dress. She helped her inside the dressing room and then turned to face Rachel with a polite smile. "What does your dress look like?"

"The bride's gown is a secret," Marta cut in, increasingly the buzz-kill. She should consider using her planning skills for more somber events, like funerals.

"Marta, we can tell my maid of honor. It's a simple A-line." Rachel contradicted her wedding planner with a wave of her hand. And then she fixed Lily with a penetrating stare. "Who would have thought you'd catch Judson Hambly?" She tsked. "I'm envious. He's talented and rich. And someday he's going to be a billionaire."

It was Lily's turn to wave off assumptions. "I love how down-to-earth Jud is. What do you love about Paulo?"

"Honestly?" Rachel ran her fingers through her thick red tresses. "I love that he treats me like a queen no matter what mood I'm in."

Lily held her breath. That didn't seem like true love.

But Rachel wasn't done. For the first time since they'd come downstairs, she seemed to glow. "I love that Paulo smiles when we hold hands, as if that alone would make him happy. I love that he's dedicated to his career. I love that he goes into beast mode when he's on the basketball court but that he's gentle as a kitten when he's with me."

That ranked among the most romantic answers Lily had ever heard.

"Kittens have claws." Grandma Dotty opened the changing room door and took a few mincing steps forward. The sight of her made everyone speechless. Grandma Dotty had put her plain white bra over the top of the strapless black dress's bodice. "I had to make adjustments because it was too loose up top. What do you think? Am I a fashion designer? Is it me?"

"No." Marta handed her the burgundy dress.

"I finally found your man cave." Jud stepped into a room with a big screen television, a mini bar, and two rows of reclining black leather chairs.

The groom had disappeared when the women had gone to try on dresses and experiment with hairstyles for the wedding.

Paulo spared Jud a quick, unwelcoming glance. He sat in the front row of seats playing *Call of Duty*.

Did he notice the way Rachel was staring at me earlier?

Jud couldn't tell. He picked up a controller from a shelf near the screen and took a seat next to the seven-footer. "I got dibs on next game."

Paulo's video game character was blown up. He released a string of curses anyone could translate. Then he said something else, presumably in Portuguese. From his tone, Jud took it to mean the big man blamed him for losing.

"That was totally not my fault." Jud let out a nervous chuckle. If the dude had eyes and a possessive bone in his body, he should be considering pummeling Jud for other reasons, also not his fault.

The big man reset the game, giving no indication of his feelings toward Jud either way.

Jud leaned forward, both hands on the controller, ready to game.

They played for a few minutes without speaking.

Jud was rusty and lost quickly. Warfare games had never been his thing. "Do you have *Madden*?" Jud knew how to put together a winning football team.

"No *Madden*," Paulo said with a superior look. "NBA."

"I guess you speak multiple languages." Portuguese, love, and video game. Jud sat back while Paulo changed the game. Maybe the big man understood more English than he was letting on. "So. You and Rachel? She's cool." This was awkward.

Paulo grunted.

"I've got to be frank with you. In English anyway." Because Jud didn't speak Portuguese and at the very least, he could tell Lily he tried to read the gauge on Paulo's love-for-Rachel meter. "This has the feel of a shotgun wedding. Like you're rushing to tie the knot when Rachel's knots only recently came undone. Is there a bun in the oven? A green card issue?" If Paulo played in the NBA, he had to know a little bit of English. He might recognize one of those words. "Go on. You can tell me."

Paulo said something in a language Jud didn't understand. He brought up the basketball video game and then paused it, stood, ducked beneath one of those ugly metal chandeliers as he went to the mini-bar. He retrieved two sparkling waters, pausing to look up at the ceiling before returning to his seat and handing Jud a bottle. "I. Love. Rachel." He glanced up at the ceiling once more.

Was he praying? Or was the honeymoon suite above them?

This was the problem with being educated by a tutor while on movie and TV sets until he took the general education test for his high school diploma. Jud hadn't learned a foreign language. He regretted it now, staring at the ceiling and the chandelier.

"Play," Paulo said.

And then Jud set aside curiosity about Paulo, because the professional basketball player was trying to wipe the floor with him in the video game.

And succeeding.

§**a**

"Are you a licensed hair stylist?" Lily had sat in the stylist chair under the assumption that Marta was going to try putting her hair in different updos.

"Even better. I'm an *experienced* hair stylist." Marta spread Lily's hair across her shoulders. "You have a delicate little face. It deserves a carefree hairstyle. Highlights. Contacts."

"No contacts," Lily said firmly, reaching to adjust her glasses.

"What about a streak of color?" Grandma Dotty had her feet soaking in the pedicure chair. "Or gothic black? Lily would make a statement with black hair. Or even red, like Rachel's."

"No," Lily said simply, but with force.

"Lily is an upstanding citizen." Rachel sat on the massage table painting her toe nails a shimmery pink that matched Marta's hair. "Scared straight into the very life she used to despise."

Lily clenched her hands together, simultaneously feeling angry and vulnerable. "So, we're finally going to address the past."

"Uh-oh," Marta muttered, fiddling with Lily's hair behind her back.

"Do you want to? Marta doesn't know our past. Dotty probably doesn't know it all either." Rachel shrugged, but it was more like an angry twitch. "Go on and say it, Lily. You hate me."

"I don't hate you." Resent, yes. Regret that there was unfinished business between them, certainly.

"I'd hate me if I were you." Rachel capped her nail polish.

Marta brushed Lily's hair ruthlessly, as if she held a grudge on Rachel's behalf.

"Ow! My hair." Lily hunched her shoulders.

"Marta, you'd never guess based on who I am today, but I was wild after my mother died. Inconsolable." Rachel hugged her knees, staring down at her toes, not waiting for Marta to acknowledge her statement before moving on with her story. "My father decided to send me away to a very strict boarding school, no cell phones, no internet access. He might just as well have sent me to prison." Her arms seemed to circle her knees in a tighter circle. "I escaped our penthouse and went to the Summer house. No one was home but Lily. I told her I was running away. She tried to talk me out of it, but instead, I talked her into running away with me."

"I had to go." That was a no-brainer for Lily. "Something could have happened to you if you went off alone." And the reality was that Lily hadn't believed Rachel was going to run farther away than the Ritz. But she hadn't been sure. Lily and Violet snuck out all the time. But they went to underground parties and poetry slams. They had destinations and were dedicated to protecting each other.

Rachel's arms loosened. She rested her cheek on one knee and stared at Lily. "I wouldn't let you take your phone. I didn't want my dad to track us. And then our purses were stolen in Times Square. We spent the first night in that shelter you like so much. The one you raise money for today."

"Hot Meals and Shelter." Lily nodded.

Grandma Dotty was all ears, as was Marta, who softened her brush strokes.

"It was a horrid place." Rachel shuddered.

"It wasn't. It isn't." Lily was as sure of it today as she'd been back then. "The women and children there are down on their luck, that's all." Their clothes and haircuts weren't to Rachel's upper class standards.

"We spent the next day in Central Park, dancing for change and flirting with guys." Rachel glossed over things like worry and thirst, making it sound like one big adventure.

Lily wondered if Rachel was going to gloss over everything. Apprehension knotted her stomach. She didn't want the details of that day to be aired in front of her grandmother. The family had protected Grandma Dotty from learning the truth. But given what Jud had told her about Rachel today, Lily was curious about her take on what had happened.

"The most adorable guy gave us a flyer." Rachel's mouth tipped up in one corner, as if remembering a sweet moment in the midst of all the unpleasantness. "He told us they were looking for cage dancers for a pop-up party that night. He said we could make hundreds in tips."

"Is cage dancing like cage fighting?" Grandma Dotty's ears perked up. "He invited you to a dance-off?"

"No," Lily blurted. "I didn't want to go."

"But I wasn't going to spend another night in that shelter. I wanted money for a hotel." Rachel's voice sharpened. "So we went and–"

"And that's where you left me," Lily choked out. "Enough said."

Rachel's chill gaze settled on Lily as her chin came up. "It was fine at first. We got money just for dancing. The cage was latched and the guys were polite."

"That's enough." Lily didn't want to hear anymore. Her breath came in ragged gasps just remembering.

"Other girls left as the night wore on." Rachel's blue eyes glittered. "But I wanted more money, so we stayed."

"And then you left me," Lily repeated, wanting her to stop.

"Lily," Grandma Dotty's expression was soft and loving, and Lily desperately didn't want her grandmother to hear any more.

"And then guys began reaching through the bars," Rachel said in an emotionless voice. "Grabbing. Tearing at our clothes and hair."

Grandma Dotty gasped.

"Stop, Rachel. Stop." Lily wheezed the words past the chokehold fear had on her throat. "Your scaring my grandmother."

"You're upsetting Lily." Grandma Dotty carefully climbed out of the pedicure chair. "And now I understand why Lily stopped being your friend, Rachel, because you left her there."

"Everybody stop talking. I made it home safe and sound." Lily pushed the lie into the universe, amazed as she always was that lightning didn't strike her down.

"As did I," Rachel said in that hard voice. "I had to convince some dude he'd get lucky if he brought me home. The doorman at our building let me in and turned him away." Rachel shook her head. "And then I wondered if Lily made it home safely."

"We're here today, talking about bridesmaid dresses and wedding hairstyles." Lily caught Marta's eye, trying to plead for an assist. "What do you suggest, Marta? I'm open for anything."

Marta hesitated, glancing toward Rachel, who was still not at a loss for words.

"Open to anything? Maybe you used to be." Rachel gave

a little mirthless laugh. "I've watched your political career, Lily. You always look and act as if the only way you can serve New York is by fitting in to the establishment, by not threatening anyone, including with your appearance. That's not open to anything." Rachel unlocked her arms and unfurled her legs. "And being so closed up keeps men outside of touching distance. It's ironic how we went through something similar and came out the other side impacted differently."

We did not go through something similar!

Lily had to unclench her jaw to defend herself, to deflect and diffuse. "I'm not going to be taken seriously in politics if I dress like I'm clubbing. Don't make my wardrobe choices more than it is." But Rachel could probably see how close to the truth she'd come.

"Wardrobe?" Rachel gave a shout of laughter. "Honey, I'm talking about the whole enchilada. All that repression, all that hiding of who you truly are must be weighing on you. You forget that I know you've got a tattoo."

"Lily has no such thing." Grandma Dotty put her hands on her hips.

There went that secret. "Actually, Grandma Dotty, I do have a tattoo." Just inside her hip where no one would ever see it, even when she wore a bathing suit. She'd gotten inked just before their purses had been stolen.

"Maybe I should get one," her grandmother mused.

Lily raised a hand, palm out. "Do not put that on your bucket list."

Grandma Dotty pouted.

"Admit it, Lily." From the intense look on her face, Rachel wasn't going to let this go. She'd become a harder woman in the past fifteen years, and it showed in her take-no-prisoners expression. "You toning-down everything has more to do with what happened to us than politics. We are both strong, fierce women who shouldn't be pushed to the back of the stage."

Lily held her tongue, thinking about what Rachel was trying to tell her, under no illusion that her former friend was bringing this up for Lily's own good. There was an agenda here. Could it be a cry for help?

"Look," Lily began. "I know who I am." And she wasn't half as brave as the seventeen-year-old girl who'd thought she could protect Rachel. "Can you say the same?"

"You aren't mom jeans and a crew neck sweater." Rachel gestured toward Lily's attire. "I'd wager not even Jud knows your true personality."

Lily wasn't taking that bet.

"He does," Grandma Dotty said staunchly. "He's seen Lily's dark side, her conflicts, and her inner soul."

Lily supposed that was true.

"Oh, you really let your hair down with him, did you?" Rachel laughed. The ripple of sound didn't invite Lily to join in the merriment. It made her put up her guard. "Prove it. Let Jud see the spontaneous, adventurous person you are inside."

That was so long ago. And now, Lily felt as if a trap was closing around her. "I would. But really. How am I supposed to do that?"

"By letting me help you shed those repressive outer layers." Rachel nodded toward Marta. "It's the least I can do for ruining your life."

Scissors snapped behind Lily. Grandma Dotty gasped.

Marta held up an eight-inch lock of brown hair. Lily's hair. She looked apologetic. "Sorry, but she doesn't just mean your clothes."

Lily reached to the nape of her neck. A fringe of hair

brushed the back of her sweater. She couldn't breathe, not even to refute the assumption that Rachel had ruined her life.

"That's not very nice." Grandma Dotty took the scissors from Marta and faced Rachel. "If your grandmother were alive, she'd be disappointed in you."

"Grandma, this is my fight," Lily said evenly, regretting taking that meeting with Abe last night.

"It's not a fight, Lily. It's an intervention. The point is to remind you how brave you used to be, how empowered." Rachel slid off the massage table and walked toward the stylist chair, extending her toes up and outward to protect her wet nails. She came to stand behind Lily and Marta, capturing Lily's gaze in the mirror with an authority she shouldn't have given she'd duck-walked over barefoot. "Or am I wrong? Is this the real you? Dull, predictable, establishment Lily? I'd be disappointed if it were, especially if you're dating Judson Hambly."

Anger prickled Lily's skin with heat. Who was Rachel to say what kind of woman Lily had or should become?

Prior to running away, Lily had never backed down from a fight or a dare. When provoked, something inside her had simmered and boiled, making Lily feel that she couldn't hold in her feelings. And having four sisters meant there was always a fight or a dare in play. But at thirty-two, she was supposed to be above petty digs and reality star trolls. So, she took a breath and a beat to compose herself.

"All right," Lily conceded after a moment. "This is your week. I'm your maid of honor. Go ahead and cut my hair if it helps get rid of your wedding jitters."

Grandma Dotty is wrong. I am a saint.

"Lily," Grandma Dotty whispered, keeping her eyes on Marta. "Are you sure?"

Lily nodded.

Her grandmother considered the scissors before addressing Marta. "I suggest you give my granddaughter a confident, sexy hairstyle. Or you may find yourself with a shaved head in the morning."

"She's joking," Lily said quickly.

"She's not." Rachel filled the room with grating laughter. "I know Dotty too well. But don't worry. Marta is good at what she does."

Being an evil henchman? Or a skilled hair stylist?

Lily hoped it was the latter.

This was turning into the cruise from hell. Given Lily's bargain, that was probably no more than she deserved.

Grandma Dotty handed the scissors over to Marta.

"Confident and sexy, you say?" Marta raised the tool in question and snipped air. "I never give up on a challenge. Move aside, grandma. I have work to do."

5

"What happened to you?" Jud stood in the doorway of Lily's cabin staring at a virtual stranger. "I mean–"

"I look gorgeous. I know." Dotty fluffed her once white, now metallic-silver, hair. "We had a spa afternoon. And after much discussion and negotiation, Lily and I decided bold changes were in order." She stepped aside, revealing Lily standing near the closet.

Her brown hair wasn't bound in a bun or spreading across her back. It was short and brushed her shoulders in a way that framed her face and complimented her chunky glasses. But she hadn't just cut her hair. She wore a short white cocktail dress and matching heels.

Sexy heels. Something inside of Jud gave a howl of appreciation.

"You hate it." Lily came to stand next to her grandmother. "Marta said she'd give me confident and sexy. Instead, she gave me–"

"Confident and sexy," Jud breathed. "You look fabulous. Both of you."

"Really?" Lily gave him a shy smile. "Marta had this dress stuffed in the back of the spa closet."

"The pantsuit is all mine." Dotty struck a pose in her black outfit. "Marta's closet in the spa downstairs is mostly full of duds, if you ask me. Kind of like the chef's attempt to make an egg salad sandwich."

"Allow me–the luckiest man on board–to escort you two beautiful creatures to dinner." He offered them each an arm.

For a few steps, they walked sideways through the hall.

"This is proof that three's a crowd." Dotty marched on ahead. "Pace yourselves. We have to climb two flights of stairs to get to the dining room."

Jud held Lily back, slowing her steps. "I need to–"

"Tell me something? Yeah. Me, too." Lily kept her voice low. "I think Rachel really loves Paulo. She said all the right things about him today. Does Paulo feel the same way?"

He hadn't stopped underneath another ghastly metal chandelier to talk about Rachel's love life. "I can't be sure about Paulo. There was a language barrier, but before we go upstairs..." Jud turned her to face him. "I need to do this." He drew Lily into his arms and kissed her thoroughly, the way that dress demanded a man kiss a woman.

Lily drew back without opening her eyes. "I understand that language." She sighed and pressed her lips to his cheek. "Unless you're acting."

Acting? Manly pride rushed through his veins. "Honey, the way you kiss, no man needs to act out his response." Lily looked dubious, so he kissed her again. "I said it before, and I'll say it again. I want to date you." She was perfect for the role of his fake girlfriend.

"Are you guys coming?" Dotty poked her head over the curved railing. "Or canoodling?"

"Canoodling," Jud called back, grinning. "Can you blame me? Lily looks ravishing."

Dotty's thready laughter trickled down to them.

"Stop with the compliments." Lily gently pushed Jud away and started up the stairs.

"It's the truth."

She paused halfway to the next floor. "Guys only want to date me for one reason."

"The pleasure of your company?"

"My political influence." Lily would have continued her march up the stairs if not for Jud capturing her hand and holding her in place.

"You're hanging around the wrong men." Jud was certain of that. "Guys who don't value a woman's sharp mind and sparkling conversation." Guys who didn't suspect that this brainy, beautiful woman could kiss a man's socks off.

Lily slowly pulled her hand free. "I'm taking days off for a chance to feed the hungry and shelter those in need. If the wedding is happening, I need to go back to New York and drum up funding elsewhere. I'll talk to Paulo at dinner in Portuguese. If he loves Rachel, we'll get off in Norfolk tomorrow morning."

"But..." *Then I'd have no excuse to kiss you.* He stuffed that thought down deep and reached instead for his cool composure. "If that's the case, you owe me two more dates in New York before I have to go back to Hollywood. Three dates is your rule. Why is there a rule?"

"Stay focused." Lily snapped her fingers multiple times the way Abe had the night before. "You want to know if what they feel for each other is real, don't you?" She sounded less caring of Rachel's feelings than she had this morning.

"Yes," Jud said carefully, studying Lily's delicately determined features for signs of stress. She'd spent the afternoon with Rachel, after all. That would beat the sympathy out of the most empathetic of souls.

"Good." She nodded briskly and proceeded upstairs, giving away none of her feelings.

They didn't talk the rest of the way to the dining room, which had four glass walls and was located behind the control bridge. Like the rest of the yacht, it was elegantly appointed except for those black metal light fixtures. They could see for miles in any direction, including forward if they looked through the glass dividing the dining room from the bridge.

Abe had finally decided to make an appearance, but his mood was as prickly as his spiky black hair. He fixed Jud and Lily with hard looks. "There's still a wedding, I see."

"Rome wasn't built in a day." Lily laid a hand on Abe's arm. "Are you sure this is necessary?"

Abe swallowed thickly before answering. "Paulo is her rebound romance. Even I know you don't marry your rebounder."

A server uncorked a bottle of white wine. Another set a tray of hors d-oeuvres on a side table.

Dotty peered at her choices on the tray and sniffed. "Still no proper egg salad. Just sushi."

"Our chef was impeccably trained in everything that matters," Abe mansplained. "They don't teach egg salad at culinary school."

"They should." Dotty sniffed again. "Food should please people, not chefs."

Lily stood at the dining room table, a faraway look in her eyes. Jud moved to her side and took her hand. Lily stared down at their linked fingers and then lifted her gaze to his.

A smile blossomed slowly on her face, a smile that Jud felt made everything about this trip better.

Just keep smiling at me, honey.

Rachel and Paulo entered, arm in arm, trailed by Marta, who looked like she'd eaten bad egg salad. Her eyes lit up when she saw Lily. He could almost swear she muttered, *"Beautiful. I'm not sorry."*

"You can let the chef know we're ready for dinner to begin," Rachel said to the bartender, settling into a chair at the head of the table, leaving the rest of them to sort out seating arrangements–Paulo, Lily and Jud on one side; Abe, Dotty and Marta on the other.

The first course was brought in–avocado and asparagus salad with lemon dressing. The contents of Jud's plate wouldn't fill the palm of his hand. This was going to be a meal of small bites meant to be marveled over. He heaved a sigh as another porter poured everyone but Dotty a glass of white wine. Jud was in the mood for a beer.

Rachel didn't waste time reflecting on the artistry of their meal or appreciating their wine choice. "Don't you think Lily looks lovely tonight, Jud?"

"She does." Jud gave all the women smiles, although Lily didn't look pleased with his praise. "All our ladies look lovely."

Paulo said something and kissed Rachel's knuckles. For not speaking the language, the guy caught on to the nuances of conversation.

"Thanks are in order to Marta." Lily gave the wedding planner a kind look across the table. "She's made my grandmother and I look and feel like spoiled princesses."

Marta actually blushed, tilting her head coyly as if unused to compliments.

"And now..." Lily raised her wine glass. "A toast to the happy couple."

Abe scoffed and drained his wine glass, holding it up to request a refill. Rachel looked suspicious.

Lily kept the conversational ball rolling. "Rachel, how did you and Paulo meet?" She glanced up at Paulo and said something in Spanish, perhaps asking him the same question.

The big man glowed and began talking rapidly.

Rachel beamed at her fiancé. "I hope he's telling you about the time he picked me out of a crowd at a dance club."

Paulo and Lily grew silent.

Jud bet good money that wasn't the memory Paulo had shared with Lily.

After a moment, Lily said something softly to Paulo that made him murmur something back and laugh.

Rachel wasn't amused. Jealousy sparked in her hard blue eyes. "What are you two talking about?"

"Um..." Lily set down her fork and dabbed at those lips Jud liked so much. "Paulo says he has two left feet, but you were so beautiful that he had to approach you."

"That's my sugar *bae*." Rachel leaned over and nipped Paulo's arm with her teeth. "I could just eat him up."

The small piece of avocado on Jud's fork fell back to his plate. Abe's cheeks reddened.

"No biting at the table," Dotty reprimanded Rachel in a calm voice, as if talking to a misbehaving toddler.

Paulo gently cradled Rachel's chin in his big hand and said something softly before planting a light kiss on her forehead.

Across the table, Dotty sighed. "I'm starting to wish this cruise was dubbed or subtitled in English. Or maybe Paulo should talk less and just worship Rachel with his eyes."

"Lily can translate," Jud said, just as curious as Dotty about what was going on.

Everyone at the table turned to Lily, who was blushing profusely.

"Paulo basically said biting is only for..." She swallowed and started over. "Like my grandmother said–no biting at the table."

Abe cleared his throat, looking as if he could use a change of subject. "Jud, tell me about your movie."

Their plates were whisked away, replaced by a shot glass of cream of turnip soup.

Jud downed his in one gulp before leaping into his pitch. "It's a coming-of-age story about the daughter of Mississippi moonshiners who must choose between her parents and the life she wants for herself." It was an interesting story that was going to require nuances in the telling.

Abe emptied his wine glass.

"Are there superheroes?" Dotty slurped her soup.

"No."

"Aliens?" The old woman slurped again.

"No."

"Serial killers?" Dotty stuck her finger in the shot glass and swiped up the last of her soup with it.

"No."

"Is it a musical?" Dotty licked her soup-coated finger clean.

"No."

"I see now why you've been having trouble getting financing." Dotty set her soup shot glass back on its tiny serving plate and wiped her hands with her napkin. "It's missing the wow factor. What do you think, Abe?"

Jud's sole investor looked like he might be having second thoughts. It only poked at Jud's existing doubts. Was he ready to direct? Should he focus on his acting career a few years more?

"I don't think our opinion matters. It's a quiet film," Lily said in Jud's defense. "A piece of Jud he feels an artistic need to express."

"Oh." Dotty blinked. "Art house."

"Yes," Jud said feeling a wave of gratitude toward Lily.

"I never watch those," Dotty said.

"More wine, please." Abe held up his class.

Rachel gave her father a speculative glance.

The next course was served. Two cherries wrapped in fried strips of duck breast and sprinkled with curry powder. It turned Jud's stomach.

Or maybe it was the reaction to his film idea.

"Don't pay attention to my grandmother's opinion about your film." Lily took Jud by the arm after the dessert course had been cleared away. She led him out the rear door of the dining room and into the crisp evening air.

The wind tugged at Lily's skirt and her hair, but it was freeing to be out of Rachel's presence and the worry about what her former friend might throw at her next. She sensed Rachel had more surprise attacks up her sleeve and she wanted no part of it. But what could she do except carry on?

Jud had yet to say anything. He'd been quiet through most of the dinner after Grandma Dotty skewered his story-line as being artsy. Since he'd been moping, Lily had taken the opportunity to speak more with Paulo.

"I'm not sure Paulo loves Rachel," Lily told her pretend boyfriend, the one who'd responded so positively to her makeover. Was that good or bad? She'd hate for Rachel to be right. "Or maybe they had a fight before dinner."

"That would explain the love bite." Jud drew her close.

Because it was cold and to keep up the dating charade, Lily snuggled into his warmth, keeping her face tilted up toward his to keep her glasses from being smashed against his chest. "Before Rachel talked about meeting at a club, Paulo told me they met at Abe's office."

"Hang on. That doesn't line up with what Rachel told us. Did he add the dancing part?"

Lily shook her head. "No. He tried to recover." He'd murmured something about forgetting the dancing. "But the entire time I spoke with him after that, he kept his answers short and to the point." The way one does when under interrogation when one has something to hide.

Grandma Dotty wasn't the only one who watched *Law & Order*.

"Is that odd or was he protecting his privacy?" Jud brought his other arm around her. "Not to change the subject, but I am. I suppose I need thicker skin if I'm going to move on the other side of the camera."

"It's just my grandmother."

"About that... Maybe she's right. My uncle says my main character is unlikable." Jud turned Lily to face him, staring down at her with doubt-filled eyes. "And my father says my ending is morally bankrupt. They're the ones pushing me to make the next jump. But maybe I'm not ready, like my agent says. He wants me to do a short film or a documentary. But maybe I'll never be ready for anything other than acting."

"Don't stress out about it. No one's ever ready for a bigger stage. So what if your script needs a rewrite? Don't they do that in Hollywood all the time?" Lily was torn between bolstering Jud's confidence and urging him to make a decision about the depth of Paulo's feelings toward Rachel. Tomorrow was another day and who knew what Rachel had planned for her. The chill wind and the dread regarding Rachel's intentions gave her a full body shiver.

Jud rubbed her arms vigorously, chasing off the cold. "I don't want to be known as the man whose ideas need rewrites."

"Okay, um..." Lily tried to think of a solution for him. "Can you ask your father or uncle to collaborate with you?"

"That's not the way we do things in our family." Jud frowned.

Lily couldn't help herself. She pressed a kiss to his lips, just to jar him out of his funk. She'd never treat a real date like this–with all the kissing. A real date might expect something more from her, something Lily wasn't ready to give. "When you need help, your family will be there." Like hers had been when she'd run away. "Back to the matter at hand. Do you think Paulo loves Rachel?"

Jud glanced back into the dining room, empty of everyone but the engaged couple. Paulo had Rachel bent over in a passionate kiss that looked like it belonged on a late night dance floor.

What would it be like to trust a man to hold her that close in a vulnerable position? Lily swallowed and looked away.

"They have chemistry." Jud returned his attention to Lily, and this time there was heat in his gaze as it dropped to her mouth. "But we have chemistry, too."

Kiss me. Kiss me. Kiss me.

Lily shivered from wanting and the cold. It was dangerous, this wanting. "It takes more than chemistry to make a relationship work. It takes compromise and understanding." Would Jud understand how she felt about intimacy? "Can you imagine Rachel compromising her life for Paulo's basketball career?" Lily was caught in Jud's gaze, hyper-aware of his lips moving closer to hers. "It'd be like you compromising your lifestyle for a relationship with me."

Jud stilled, drew back. "What do you mean?"

"I…" Lily wished she could take back the words.

Jud continued to look hurt. "How would I have to change my life if I wanted to date you?"

I was almost raped when I was seventeen. I'm not going to jump into bed with you.

The words stuck in Lily's throat, held back by shame. "I don't…um…" The conversation had veered. Lily was still in his arms, but Jud felt so distant, as if he'd moved to the other side of the deck. "You seem like the kind of man who enjoys the company of women." She grimaced. Could she make it any clearer?

"Sleep around, you mean." His arms around her loosened, his words constricted, dropping between them like sharp objects. "Sleep around with no emotional connection, you mean. What kind of a man do you think I am?"

Inwardly, Lily cringed. This was a perfect example of why Lily didn't date. She couldn't be upfront about the pace she needed in the physical side of a relationship. And then men always got touchy.

"Lily," he snapped. "What kind of a man–"

"I don't know," Lily said miserably. She hated her repressed tone of voice. She hated that Rachel had been right about her. It was so much easier to avoid relationships. But she was tired of it all. Tired of holding back her feelings, her anger, her identity.

Lily lifted her chin and strengthened her voice. "And the reason I don't know is because I don't know you." And there it was. The reality of this ruse. They could pretend to be lovers, but the truth was there in every conversation. "We're strangers. What I know of you, I've learned from gossip magazines. Are you going to tell me that's not true? You don't get to pick and choose the women who're thrown at your feet? I'm so sorry if I've misjudged you. I'm so sorry if I consider myself the kind of woman who doesn't give out kisses until the second or third date. I'm so sorry if I don't sleep with a guy until we've dated for a couple of months. I'm a prude by your standards and that of most men. And that's why you and dozens of other men I've met would never consider dating me. Your lifestyle is instant gratification and I...I have to trust a guy. Implicitly." Lily sagged against him, exhausted by her tirade. But there she was, putting herself out there the way Violet and Rachel seemed to think she needed to.

"Wow. I..." Jud ran a hand through his dark hair. "Wow. Three dates... Three chances... And it's over."

They stared at each other.

"You honestly think I'd dump you rather than wait until you're ready?" He watched her intently.

"Like I said, I don't know you, but...The many men who've come before you have proven my point." Lily had never been this upfront with a man. Never. And because of that, she expected Jud to do what all men before him had done. Turn his back and say goodnight.

"It's cold out here." Jud held her hand and led her toward the dining room door. "And I promised Dotty I'd sing show tunes with her in the hot tub."

It wasn't exactly a brush-off. But it wasn't not one either. Lily dragged her feet. "Count me out. I have emails and calls to return."

"That suits me just fine." He paused at the door, his expression stiff and stony. "In fact, we should stick to your plan and pretend to be lovers one more day. I don't want to make you uncomfortable."

A chasm opened up between them and Lily hated it. She wanted them to be on the same page the way they'd been this morning. Small touches and shared confidences without pressure for more. "You haven't been making me uncomfortable."

Perhaps some of that longing came through her words or showed on her face, because Jud's expression softened. "Look, if you really want to get to know me, meet me at midnight in the hot tub."

Yes!

No!

Lily clung to his hand, letting him lead her through the dining room, past Rachel and Paulo in a heated embrace, down the stairs and to her room.

And all the while, Lily kept wondering if she could open up and let Jud know her better.

"I'm singing in the rain," Dotty warbled in the hot tub.

Jud wasn't in the mood to sing, still reeling from Lily's opinion of him–*even she thinks I'm a man with one thing on his mind.* **He shed his white, plush terrycloth robe and stepped in the hot tub, nearly leaping back out. "Hey! This isn't that hot."**

Dotty stopped singing. "The older you get, the colder the hot tub. Medications, health complications, vascular integrity. It's set to the temperature of warm bath water which is still invigorating given the ocean breeze."

86 MELINDA CURTIS

The hot tub was in the bow on the lounge level, sheltered slightly from the wind by high walls and sheltered from prying eyes on the bridge above.

"You look like someone stole your favorite action figure." Dotty's short, dyed silver hair was limp against her head. Her facial structure was delicate and refined, telling of great beauty in her youth. "Trouble in paradise?"

"Your granddaughter believes my press." He got into the hot tub, sinking down to his chin.

"That you're a talented lothario with a hot body?" Dotty chuckled.

"Yes." When put that way, Jud wanted to laugh. "Can't a man enjoy the perks of his status when he's young?"

"That's your right. But when you meet that special someone, a past like yours makes it harder to believe that you're ready to settle down." Dotty pushed water back and forth with one hand. "I suppose that's why everyone doubts Rachel's love for Paulo. She's led a wild life, too."

"Do you think they're in love?"

Dotty tilted her head from side to side, as if weighing the facts. "No. However, I think few people nowadays are in *forever love* when they get married. They come to the union with a measure of love for each other and the assumption that their love will blossom as they grow as individuals. But the high divorce rate tells me they're more likely to grow apart than together."

"That's grim."

"Is it?" Dotty swirled the water with bigger strokes. "Or does it take commitment to hang in there through the rocky and uncertain times so that love will deepen and last? If commitment nurtures love, how can someone believe a commitment-phobe like yourself or Rachel is in love?"

That gave Jud pause. "Who are you? And what have you

done with Dotty Summer?" Because this wasn't the same woman who'd stolen a phone charger from Abe and wrapped it around her waist.

Dotty laughed, a thin, delicate sound that was becoming endearing to him. "I'll let you in on a secret. For a few hours every day when I'm invigorated, I feel like me."

"And the rest of the time?"

"I feel like I've lost touch with myself." Frowning, Dotty splashed Jud with a very small amount of water. "Now, can we perform *The Music Man* start to finish? Tomorrow night, I'll let you choose the show."

"Sure. But we won't finish until close to midnight." Nearly two hours. "Are you okay with that? We're going to be waterlogged by the time we're through."

"Yes." Dotty splashed him again. "But we'll be so very happy."

And oddly enough, he believed her.

6

"Marion the Librarian has arrived." Jud sat in the steamy hot tub facing the door, not that Lily could discern his features without her glasses on. But she recognized his voice, hoarse as it was.

"Harold Hill." Lily greeted Jud as the character he'd played on Broadway, the love interest of Marion. "You made my grandmother's year by singing *The Music Man* with her." Lily was wrapped up in a terrycloth bathrobe, reluctant to disrobe. "No one will ever be able to top that."

"Your grandmother is one-of-a-kind. We had a conversation that blew me away." Jud stared at her, as if he couldn't look away.

That's my imagination talking. She couldn't see his exact expression without her glasses.

Still, the idea that he couldn't take his eyes off her made Lily continue to clutch her robe. She dug her fingers deeper into the thick terrycloth. "Thank you for being patient with my grandmother. It's hard to witness her losing her grip with reality."

"Oh, no. Our conversation was very real." Jud stood,

holding out his hands toward Lily. "But frankly, I was glad when the singing was over, and I could turn up the hot tub temperature. Come here. I'm not going to bite."

Whether he was a biter or not wasn't the issue. The issue was that Lily regretted not wearing her glasses. The issue was that she had to imagine his torso looked like he spent hours in the gym and never ate carbs instead of seeing the real deal. The issue was that she wanted his kisses and nothing more.

Men labeled women like that a tease.

But she hadn't come this far to run away. Rachel had practically dared her to reclaim her youthful courage. So Lily came forward, placing her hands in his. His touch was soft and warm, although his fingers felt wrinkled.

Human.

Not perfect. Not intimidating.

"Tell me you have bad hair days," she blurted. *Tell me you're not perfect and you don't expect me to be either.*

Jud chuckled. "Everybody has bad hair days. And bedhead. My morning bedhead is frightening." He squeezed her hands. "Do you know why I wanted to ask you out?"

She tried to joke. "You're tired of swiping right?"

Jud didn't even laugh. "What you said earlier about image and respectability...It struck a chord. The same chord that has been playing in my head since I decided I wanted to do more than act and encountered one roadblock after another because the world apparently doesn't believe I'm a grown-up."

"So you looked to me, a mature-looking woman." The evening took on a less than romantic tone.

Before Lily could say anything more, Jud swung her into his arms and into the hot tub.

Water splashed everywhere–over her, over him, over the edge. Her hair was drenched, ruining Marta's hairstyle.

Jud cradled her in his lap, the ends of her soaked bathrobe dragging her toward the bottom. "Adult me looked across the room at Lily Summer and wanted to learn more about her. But…" Jud moved his lips closer to her ear. "I'm still the same Judson Hambly who recognizes the sizzle of sexual attraction. You have it all. Brain and body. Smarts and sexy. It's not every day I ask a woman out. Believe me when I say it." And then he finally stopped talking and put his money where his mouth was–kissing her like he'd been impatiently waiting to do so.

When they came up for air, her robe was on the bottom of the hot tub and Lily's hands were on Jud's firm, bare chest. Who needed to see that hard body when she could feel it?

"I'm so glad that grown-up you appreciates mature women in glasses," Lily whispered, knowing that now was the time to tell him more about her past before he pressed for more than kisses. "I need to–"

"Why wouldn't I appreciate you? Adore you and your glasses? I'll tell you a secret." His lips moved over the shell of her ear. "When I'm not wearing contacts, I wear really thick glasses."

Lily sucked in a breath. He was perfect. "Kiss me, Talon." *Rescue me from my own self-doubt.*

Jud obeyed Lily's command.

"Never apologize for being mature or smart or wearing glasses." Jud tangled his fingers in the hair at the back of Lily's neck and then he kissed her some more. Long, hot, drugging kisses that made her forget everything but him.

"Jud, we should–"

"Hello." Paulo stood next to the hot tub, shedding his bathrobe, revealing a bright red Speedo.

"*Eep.*" Mortification had Lily scrambling off Jud's lap and gathered her soaked bathrobe from the bottom. She stood and held it in front of her chest. "We were just...*leaving.*" She climbed out, dropped her wet robe on the deck, grabbed a towel from a nearby cupboard, and wrapped it around herself. Belatedly, she realized Paulo may not have understood her statement, so she repeated it in Spanish while Jud joined her on the deck.

Paulo sunk into the tub, legs long enough to extend his feet to the other side. "*Yes, you need air.*"

You? Did he mean him?

Lily was too shaken to examine his words.

Jud wrapped a towel around his waist, and then covered Lily with his dry bathrobe, and hustled her out the door.

"Did you hear that?" Lily asked Jud in hushed tones when they reached the stairs. "Paulo said he needed air. Like Rachel was suffocating him. I think..."

"You think?" Jud padded down the stairs, drawing Lily with him. "Are you saying that because that's what you want to believe because feeding the hungry is on the line? Or are you saying that because that's the exact translation?"

Was her opinion colored by her desire to fulfill her contract with Abe? The feeling of uncertainty about Paulo's words returned. And then Jud pulled her to a stop and nibbled on the back of her neck. Lily stiffened taking a few quick steps out of reach. "I should get off the boat tomorrow. This is how it starts."

"How what starts?"

Expectations between us. Lily couldn't get those words out. She executed a mental pivot, as she had so often before with men. "Politicians get made deals like this and their actions and perspective becomes less clear."

Jud scoffed. "This has nothing to do with you being a politician. You're scared of Rachel. She only has power over you if you give it to her." He sounded like Violet.

"Forget Rachel." Lily's steps slowed as they neared her cabin. "This deal we made with Abe... My gut's telling me to cut my losses."

"You'd leave me?" His heart was in his gaze, soft and as blue as a spring sky.

"Yes." She didn't want to stay. There were pitfalls everywhere. And yet, a bit of courage made her admit, "But I'd rather you left with me."

"I can't leave. Not yet. Stay," he pleaded softly, whispering in her ear. "Stay on board at least through our planned break up. This is like one really, long date. Emphasis on one." He kissed her neck and then kissed her as if he couldn't stand not to. When he finally drew back, he said two words, "Stay. Please."

Lily knew if she stayed that she'd regret it. She was in danger of falling for him, despite their relationship being a ruse. She knew she wasn't the right woman to win the heart of the world famous Judson Hambly. "I don't know how I'm going to sleep tonight."

"If you can't sleep, knock on my door." Jud brushed aside her hair and pressed a light kiss to her lips. "I like kissing you, Lily. But I like talking to you more." He grinned. "*Maybe* I like talking to you more than kissing you. The jury's still out."

It was indeed. Lily watched him enter his cabin, heard his door click shut. And still she leaned against her door, worried about what tomorrow would bring.

❧

Lily's phone began announcing text and chat messages before six a.m.

She put a pillow over her head for the next twenty minutes, ruing the fact that she'd turned her phone on after dinner and left it charging in the bathroom. She shut her eyes and tried to fall back to sleep.

No such luck.

"Lily, I know you won't believe this, but I need my beauty rest." Grandma Dotty rolled over. "Silence your cell phone."

Lily got up, put on her glasses, and began checking her messages.

From her assistant Nina: *How do you want to handle this?* She'd attached a link and several follow up messages which basically were asking Lily the same thing: *Do we have a comment?* Lily assumed a picture of she and Jud leaving the benefit the other night had finally gone viral. She went to the next message.

From Violet: *Tell me where you are.* She'd attached a link, too, and followed up the link with more questions about Lily being okay or needing the cavalry. Lily ignored the link, now assuming two pictures were circulating–the one after the animal rescue benefit and the one taken at the dock yesterday.

From Dad: *Tell me this isn't you.* He'd included a link, which was unusual for him, and then added increasingly agitated queries about her safety. But he sounded judgy, as if she'd done something wrong. This time, Lily clicked on the link.

The first thing she saw was the headline: *Titanium Talon Makes Summer Heat.*

Lily scrolled down, took in the picture, dropped her phone, and screamed.

Grandma Dotty sat up. "Who died?"

"It's not who died. It's who's going to die." Lily snatched up her phone and scrolled through the rest of the post. "It says stay tuned for more exclusive pictures. Gah!"

Footsteps pounded down the hallway. Someone pounded on the door.

Blood pounded in Lily's temples. *What am I going to do? I'll be the laughingstock of the state house.*

"Lily? Dotty? Who screamed?" It was Jud.

Lily tugged on the still damp terry bathrobe from last night and opened the door. "Tell me how this happened?" She turned her phone screen toward him.

It was a picture of them kissing outside this very door last night.

This very door.

Lily pulled Jud inside. The ocean wasn't moving the yacht the way it had last night. They'd docked. "We're in Norfolk? Good. We're getting off the boat." She began returning messages.

To Nina: *No comment.*

To Violet: *We docked in Norfolk. Grandma Dotty and I are on the Cohen yacht. We'll arrive in Charleston tomorrow. Don't worry. You told me to get a life. I'm okay.*

To Dad: *It isn't me.*

But it was her. And she didn't want Jud to think what everyone who saw that picture assumed–that if they hadn't slept together yet, they were going to.

"What's going on?" Grandma Dotty got out of bed and put on her bathrobe. "Nice glasses, Clark Kent."

Lily had barely registered Jud's specs when he'd come in. They were a lot like hers.

"What am I going to do?" Lily showed her grandmother the photo.

"Why do you have to explain anything?" Jud was angry, pacing the small room with heavy steps. "We're dating."

"We're not dating," Lily said coldly.

"It looks like it to me." Dotty went into the small bathroom. "The question is who took the picture?"

"It was after midnight." Jud stomped around. "There was no one out but Paulo unless..." He rushed out to the hallway and then darted back in, slamming the door. "There's a camera out there, hidden in a hideous metal light fixture. The same style light that's in every public space on this yacht."

"*Abe*," Lily ground out. "He just remodeled, remember? Get dressed. We need to confront him and then leave. He has no right."

"He has every right." Jud tried to put his arm around Lily. "We signed away rights to pictures."

"I assumed he meant wedding pictures." She brushed him off. "Are you on his side now?" So much for Hot Meals and Shelter being secure for another year. "What happened to settling down and dating with a future in mind? This looks like you haven't settled down at all!"

"Are you dating or not?" Grandma Dotty wrinkled her brow. "I'm so confused.

"We're dating," Jud said through gritted teeth.

"We only planned on dating until tomorrow." Lily glared at Jud. "But this changes everything."

"Oh. Couples create dating plans now." Grandma Dotty smoothing Lily's hair over her ears, using both hands while murmuring, "*Bedhead.*" And then she crossed her skinny arms. "What happens in twenty-four hours? Does Jud propose? Do you upgrade to fiancée?"

Jud pushed his glasses up his nose. "She agrees to meet my parents."

"That's not likely." Lily huffed even though a tiny voice in her head went, *"Squee!"*

"I didn't think you were a quitter," Jud said, still in that tight, angry voice.

Lily tried not to let that go to her head. She'd like to quit, more than anything.

"This has to do with the cage dancing, doesn't it?" Grandma Dotty sat on her bed, a morose expression on her face. "You don't want people to think that's who you are. Oh, my dear, sweet girl. That's not how the world works."

"Cage dancing?" Jud quirked his brows. "Did I miss something?"

"No." Lily didn't want to tell him about her past, so she hid in her future. "I serve on committees for the state for children and families, for health, and for education. I want to move to the ethics and guidance committee. And someday, I want to be the first female mayor of New York City." That hadn't come out as strongly as she'd have liked. Regardless... "Pictures like this aren't going to help me do any of that."

"But they might help you get re-elected." Jud tapped his chest with his thumb. "*I* might help you get re-elected. If you date me, more people will know your name."

"He's got a point," Grandma Dotty shook her finger at Lily. "But you're glossing over the past. And you shouldn't. Not when you've got a dating plan with Jud."

"She's right. We're in this together." Jud took Lily by the shoulders and gave her a gentle shake. "It's one picture, babe. And we were fully clothed."

Lily shook her head. "You were in a towel and I was in a bathrobe."

"Tell him," Grandma Dotty urged. And by the determined look on her face, Lily assumed if she didn't obey that her grandmother would spill the beans.

"Okay." Lily gave Jud a condensed version of the runaway events.

"What happened between the time Rachel left and you came back home?" Leave it to Jud to notice the gap in Lily's story.

"I made my way home." Lily held out her hands. "Can we focus on the picture problem? Abe sold that photograph. What's to keep him from selling another?" If a hot tub picture went viral... Lily shook her head, dropping her hands before Jud noticed they were shaking. "Pack your things, Grandma. We're leaving." Before the situation got worse.

And there were so many ways it could get worse.

"That's not the way to handle this." Jud put his arm around Lily. "We have to control the narrative. And to do that, we have to think logically about who would release that picture. It wasn't Abe. What does he have to gain from it?"

"You think it's Rachel." Lily slid from his side and slapped a hand to her forehead. "Of course, it's Rachel. Her and that stupid intervention. She must know something isn't right about us dating. Look at us. No one would pair us together."

"I would," Grandma Dotty said.

"I would, too," Jud insisted. "Rachel probably knows Abe doesn't want her to get married again and that we were the only suckers to show. She probably realizes we're only here for the paycheck and she resents us...*you*."

"Aha!" Grandma Dotty pointed at Lily. "And that's what *Law and Order* calls motive."

A feeling of doom filled Lily's chest. "If Rachel knows we're trying to stop the wedding, she's not going to stop with one picture. I mean, the web site said *stay tuned for more.* Rachel has more access to gossip sites than all of us combined. And last night...The hot tub."

"One of those ugly lights is there, too." Jud nodded grimly. "Do you think they have audio?"

"She better not." Lily growled in frustration. She did a quick, mental replay of the night's highlights and grabbed Jud's arm. "Hang on. Last night when Paulo showed up...I thought I heard him wrong when he said *you need air.* I thought he was saying he needed space. But he must have meant *you* as in you and me. You two need air." Away from the camera.

Jud's expression turned thunderous. "If he saw us in the hot tub–"

"He also enjoyed a musical rendition of *The Music Man.*" Grandma Dotty stared into the distance, smiling. "That must have been entertaining."

Lily wasn't smiling. "Should I thank Paulo for intervening or slug him for being a voyeur?"

Jud was breathing heavily. "Let me strike the first blow."

"Instead of fisticuffs, make him pay for attending our performance." Grandma Dotty still had her head in the clouds. "I think a few hundred dollars is fair, don't you?"

Lily put her hands over her ears.

Jud promptly removed them. For some reason, he was smiling. "Rachel has tipped her hand. She'll expect one of two things. Either you running away with your tail between your legs..."

Lily released another growl.

"...or retaliation. She'd expect us to strike back against her, but..."

Lily had never thought he looked more gorgeous than in that moment. "What devious plan is forming in that handsome head of yours?"

His grin expanded. "There's a point in every underdog movie where the underdog vows to stay in the fight."

"I don't like where this is heading," Lily said, suspecting he wanted her to act.

"I don't *know* where this is heading," Grandma Dotty said.

Jud brought them in closer, close enough to hear him whisper, "We came here to stop a wedding–"

"And get paid," Dotty added.

"–and that photo is daring us to stop a wedding."

"And get paid," Grandma Dotty added again.

Lily wasn't ready to play along. "But if they love each other..."

Jud straightened, frowning. "Don't tell me you still believe love is behind this marriage. Paulo came to our rescue last night. That means he isn't Rachel's puppet."

"And only a puppet would earn her so-called love." Lily was finally on board. "Okay, what's your plan?"

There was hope for Hot Meals and Shelter yet.

7

"I've always wanted to ride on one of these water motorcycles." Dotty sat on one of the two jet skis in the rear boat garage of the yacht. "Who's going with me?" She wore a life preserver and a crash helmet.

Jud didn't want to speculate where she'd gotten the helmet. He pretended not to hear her and buckled Lily into her life vest.

It had been a gamble to assume that Rachel wouldn't want to ride the watercraft. They'd dodged her this morning, breakfasting early and then sending a porter to Paulo with an invitation to join them for some water sport.

Interrogation, Dotty called it.

"Paulo!" Dotty patted the seat behind her. "Be my man."

That was Lily's cue.

"Paulo." Lily smiled at the groom and said something in Spanish, supposedly a request to take care of her grandmother.

Paulo grinned and nodded, apparently agreeing to ride with Dotty. He sat behind the old gal, extended his long arms around her shoulders to start the engine. He had no idea what was in store for him, and Jud had no sympathy.

"We race once we're in the open water, Jud." Dotty should have been an actress. She dove right into her role of competitive grandma in need of a chaperone. "Don't keep me waiting."

"We won't," Lily promised.

A crew member unhooked the tie-line and pushed them free. Paulo backed the jet ski into the water, and then shifted gears, disappearing from view.

Jud sat on the other jet ski. Lily got on behind him, wrapping her arms around his waist. Having her hold him was an unexpected benefit of their plan. He pressed a hand briefly over hers. She was incredibly brave. There was more to her teenage runaway story and when the time was right, he wanted to hear it. Jud was convinced that whatever had happened in her past was why she wanted a relationship with a man that progressed slowly. Three dates? Fat chance he'd settle for three dates.

Once they were untied and pushed back, Jud started the engine and backed out.

"If anything happens to my grandmother…"

"She'll be fine." Jud hoped. "She volunteered, after all."

Dotty and Paulo had a head start, driving slowly out of the marina toward the open water. Jud followed them.

A few minutes later and they were outside the slow zone, pulling up next to Dotty and Paulo. No other boats were headed in or out of the marina. The ocean swells were only about two feet high. Waves broke in the narrow section of the inlet leading out to the open water.

"Are you ready to race, Jud?" And then without waiting for an answer, Dotty elbowed Paulo's arms away and gunned it. Full throttle and sea water. Her head snapped back, and her helmet connected with the big man's head.

Paulo tumbled off the back and into the water, just as they'd planned. Only without the head butt.

Jud couldn't quite believe it. Now was the time to get some answers.

"How did I get water on my sunglasses?" Lily removed them and tried to wipe them on Jud's lifejacket. They must have been prescription lenses because Lily could see with them on. "Are you okay?" Lily asked the floating basketball player as Jud drove in a slow circle around him, signaling to other boaters that a man was in the water.

Paulo said something in Portuguese that didn't sound happy. A lump rose on his forehead.

"I'm sure she didn't mean it," Lily lied and then made a show of calling her grandmother back.

Dotty didn't turn around. In fact, she shouted gleefully as she raced off toward cresting waves.

"Oh, no. I was afraid this might happen." Lily stood, holding on to Jud's shoulder and waving her free hand. "Grandma! Grandma!"

The old girl probably couldn't hear Lily. Dotty was plowing through waves like a pro, speeding farther and farther out to sea.

"Are you sure she's never done this before?" Even Jud wouldn't attempt some of those waves.

"When it comes to my grandmother, I'm not sure of anything." Lily called after her grandmother once more. When Paulo said something, she snapped, "Of course, the water is cold. It's spring in the Atlantic. Suck it up. My grandmother is in trouble." She made a sound of annoyance and then spoke in Spanish, before adding to Jud, "I forgot to translate."

Paulo waved them off, as if giving them his blessing to chase after Dotty.

Jud couldn't leave Paulo bobbing in the lane going in and out of the marina. It wasn't safe. Their plan was falling apart.

"She's turning around." Lily's words were colored with relief. She continued to stand while Jud circled Paulo. "Finally."

Paulo's lips looked blue.

"Thanks for the warning last night." Jud continued to circle. "Although we could have used a warning about the cameras, specifically the one in the hallway."

Paulo didn't say anything, but he didn't look confused about the meaning of Jud's words either.

Meanwhile, Dotty was getting air off the waves coming back into the inlet. "Yee-haw!"

"She's giving me a heart attack." Lily swung her arm back and forth again. "Grandma, slow down!"

If anything, the old woman sped up.

And headed straight toward Paulo.

"She's not going to stop," Lily cried, trying to wave her off.

Jud brought his jet ski in her path, idling in the way. Surely, she wouldn't plow into her granddaughter.

Dotty veered at the last minute, barely missing their craft and careening ten feet from Paulo before she released the throttle. "These babies can move!"

"You nearly killed me!" Paulo shouted, earning everyone's attention.

"Aha! You *can* speak English." Lily sat behind Jud.

Cursing, Paulo swam toward Dotty's jet ski.

"Shame on you for pretending to be something you're

not," Dotty chastised. "I thought you had more class than that, young man."

Jud brought his jet ski next to Dotty's and put a foot on her craft's bumper so that Paulo wouldn't tip Dotty over while trying to get back on board.

"The jury's still out on Paulo's classiness," Lily said darkly. "Is Rachel making you lie to us?"

"No." Paulo gingerly touched his rising bruise. Despite the sun being out, his skin was pebbled with goosebumps. "We speak her love language. It is better this way."

"Better for who?" Lily seemed just as angry as she'd been earlier this morning upon discovering that picture of their kiss.

"My bride." Paulo gestured toward Jud. "You understand me, no? It is sometimes better not to fight."

"Um...no." Jud shook his head. "Not like this. You're living a lie."

Dotty craned her neck to see Paulo behind her. "It's hard to fight if one person assumes you won't understand them."

"But yes. This. That is why I do it." Paulo patted Dotty's shoulder. "I love Rachel. Rachel loves me."

Jud wasn't buying it.

"And you don't think Rachel would love you if she knew you could speak English?" Lily didn't wait for him to answer. "That isn't love."

"I love her," Paulo said staunchly. "We will go places together."

"That isn't a marriage. It's a business arrangement." Jud pushed away from Dotty's jet ski. "Wasn't that what happened with her last marriage? We should go back and tell her. She'll cancel the wedding and then we can all go home."

"No." Paulo looked torn. "Please. Everything rests on our uniting."

"Everything?" Jud was all over that. "Your heart and..."

"My contract with the Badgers." Paulo didn't look happy with his admission. "Rachel is good at deal-making."

"That's no surprise." Lily leaned her forearm on Jud's shoulders. "Rachel was a business major before she dropped out to star in reality TV. And I heard she was the highest paid cast member on *Slaying*."

"That's because she's been on the show the longest." Dotty beamed, apparently forgetting Rachel had hurt Lily this morning by selling that hot picture. "And that's because Rachel stirs up trouble even though she tells it to folks straight, even if it hurts."

"She's like that in real life, too," Lily muttered.

"I love her," Paulo said staunchly, touching his bruise once more. "Don't tell."

"I won't," Dotty promised. "But only if I can ride around some more."

"No!" they all chorused, even Paulo.

Dotty huffed. "I never have any fun."

An idea began forming in Jud's head. "I tell you what, Paulo. We'll keep your secret–"

"*What?*" Lily poked Jud's arm.

"–if you convince Rachel to stop harassing Lily." Because that post had said more exclusive pictures of he and Lily were coming.

"No." Lily poked Jud's arm a few more times. "We'll keep Paulo's secret if he cancels or postpones the wedding."

"Protecting you is more important," Jud insisted.

"It's not." Lily gave his shoulders a little shake.

"I reject your offers." Paulo grinned, pointing to a couple fishing off the back of a boat nearby. "We will fish. If I catch the biggest fish, you keep my secret. And if you catch the biggest fish, you will keep my secret."

Dotty scoffed, half turning on the jet ski. "Heads I win, tails you lose? Not a chance. I wasn't born yesterday."

"No deal." Jud shook his head. "You have nothing to bargain with."

"But I do." Paulo's normally open expression turned sly as a fox. "Rachel recorded you and your agent-man the day we left."

Jud did a quick mental review of his conversation with Darian. They'd argued about his role as Titanium Talon versus directing. They'd argued about Jud toning down his appearance in the gossip magazines. And they'd argued about him fake dating someone who was...

He'd talked about Lily in unflattering terms.

Jud glanced over his shoulder at Lily. Her eyes were wide and curious behind those water-spotted lenses. But her gaze wasn't just inquisitive. There was trust in her eyes.

Jud had argued with Darian about dating someone safe and mundane, having an on-call, fake girlfriend who didn't tempt him or the media. He'd thought Lily was that woman, but she wasn't like that at all. She was full of surprises. Jud didn't want her to know the truth about why he'd approached her in the first place. She'd still be a fantastic boost to his new image, but there was the nagging suspicion that he wanted to date her for real. "Okay, we fish. If I catch the biggest fish, we'll keep your secret if you'll protect Lily."

"When I catch the biggest fish, you will keep my secret *and* make Rachel happy." Paulo sat up tall, puffing out his chest. "Of course, I will win. I grew up in a fishing village. I am an excellent fisherman."

"I don't like this." Lily leaned around to look Jud in the

eye. "Rachel will only be happy when she's married to Paulo."

"Don't be so sure." Jud headed the jet ski back to the yacht. "I think what makes Rachel happy changes as often as your grandmother's bucket list."

§

"Daddy's working in his suite," Rachel told them during lunch after they'd set sail for Charleston. "He and his expectations make me so tense. People who judge me trigger my inner biotch."

In truth, Rachel looked more relaxed to Lily than anytime during the trip other than when they'd discussed Aviator's costume. Lily suspected it wasn't Abe's absence, but the deal Paulo and Jud had struck. They were all pretending everything was fine and that they were all good friends. No betrayals in their past or their future. But there was a tension at the table, evidenced by the rigidity of Lily's posture and the blackening bump on Paulo's head.

"I used to enjoy that trigger on your show." Grandma Dotty drank from her ice water. "I don't think I'm gonna anymore."

"Not watch my show?" Rachel's brow crinkled. "Are you judging me?"

"Nope." Grandma Dotty fluffed her helmet-smashed, silver locks. "I'm just over it."

"Like my producer said," Rachel murmured.

Lily snuck a glance at Jud. He was devouring his lunch as if he had no secrets. Lily knew that wasn't true. He'd cut a deal with Paulo. What had Jud said to his agent on one of Rachel's cameras that he didn't want to come to light? Jud had slanted a glance toward Lily when Paulo issued the threat. Why? How could a conversation with his agent hurt or upset Lily? It had raised her guard.

Lily's only true ally was her grandmother, who'd told the porter she'd stick to the green salad, foregoing the main course of duck confit with spicy pickled raisins in favor of her continued request for an egg salad sandwich. Grandma Dotty could be so random, popping in and out of reality without notice.

In other words, Lily had no dependable allies when it came to a defense against Rachel.

Rachel picked at her duck and her allies. "Marta, I don't know why you didn't bring more cutting edge designer pieces on this trip. My wardrobe is pathetic." She wore bright, geometric pattern capris and a yellow off-the-shoulder blouse. She looked fantastic.

Lily took in her simple white jeans and teal sweater set with a sigh. She glanced across the table at Marta. "I, for one, loved the options you brought. I recognized Stella McCartney's latest spring collection, as well as Christian Siriano."

That earned a grateful smile from Marta and a disparaging sniff from Rachel. Lunch was finished on a relatively quiet note. Rachel and Marta went below to work on wedding details while the others traipsed down to the boat garage for the fishing wager to begin.

Chairs and blankets were brought out for the spectators. A porter provided Jud and Paulo with fishing rods and live bait.

"What do you think they'll catch?" Lily settled into a chair, put a blanket over her lap, and adjusted her prescription sunglasses. "Tuna? Marlin?"

"Whatever it is, I hope Jud's is bigger." Grandma Dotty adjusted her lap blanket with one hand, while holding onto her wide-brimmed straw hat with the other. She caught the porter's eye. "When can I expect my egg salad sandwich?"

"I'll check on it now." The porter disappeared.

"No cameras here." Paulo deftly put a strip of raw fish on his hook. "I will bait yours, Jud, if you–"

"No more deals. Just bait my hook." Jud frowned at his opponent. "And then show me what to do."

"Jud's a fishing virgin." Dotty chuckled. "You'll have to show him how to cast a line, Paulo."

"Not that it will help him." Paulo demonstrated, casting gracefully, letting out more line when his hook was in the water.

Jud's cast wasn't as graceful, but it did the trick since he didn't hook anything in or on the boat.

"And now we wait." Grandma Dotty slid on a pair of pink flamingo-framed sunglasses.

"I'm surprised you haven't put deep sea fishing on your bucket list," Lily said.

"Why would I do that? It's boring."

"It is zen." Paulo smiled at them over his shoulder.

Grandma Dotty tsked, not to be swayed. "Boring. Dull. A test of one's ability to stay awake." And then she leaned back and closed her eyes. "Wake me up if anything happens."

Nothing happened.

After a few minutes of the fishermen shifting their feet and fiddling with their poles, the porter returned with a plate. He extended it toward Grandma Dotty. "Ma'am, your sandwich."

Grandma Dotty blinked sleepy eyes before sitting up. "*Ew*. What is that? Egg salad isn't red."

"The chef blended it with ground beets and chopped pimento." The porter held the plate closer to her.

Grandma Dotty shooed him away. "Try again."

The porter swallowed thickly, staring at the sandwich. "Don't make me return it. The chef will be livid."

"He won't be mad if you eat it," Lily suggested to the porter, trying to make peace. "We won't tell."

"But I still want a good old, plain egg salad sandwich." Grandma Dotty slid her sunglasses lower on her nose and fixed the porter with a hard look. "Don't make me put that on my bucket list."

The porter retreated, looking none too happy with his options.

The ocean was calm. The sky a rich blue. And two handsome men stood holding their fishing poles. Lily supposed there were worse views, but she couldn't shake the feeling that she had another surprise in store for her today. It didn't help that Rachel was off doing what she pleased. And if attacking Lily was what pleased her under the guise of intervention, Paulo wasn't in a position to protect Lily.

"This is like watching paint dry." Grandma Dotty got to her feet. "I loved riding a jet ski this morning. But do you know what else is on my bucket list? Driving a yacht."

"I'm sure you can go up and ask the captain if you can take the wheel." Lily was confident the captain wouldn't let her.

"I bet I can have a turn at steering the boat and get back here before our gentlemen catch a fish."

"Don't take that bet," Jud advised Lily. "I felt something strike my line."

"Ha! Challenge accepted." Grandma Dotty hurried off toward the stairs.

Lily's phone pinged. Someone had tagged her on social media. She clicked on the app and... "You've got to be kidding me."

"What?" Jud said without turning around.

"Rachel just posted a *"Who wore it better?"* meme featuring herself and me." Lily's photo was a bit grainy and of her wearing the white cocktail dress from last night. Rachel's photo was of her in the same dress, but she was on the red carpet and glammed up with a matching handbag and dangly earrings. "Jud, you need to catch a big fish." Lily got up and showed both men the post. "Or I'm getting off in Charleston." She was being hit with an all-out media blitz. The only thing stopping Lily from confronting Rachel was the deal she'd made with Abe.

"How juvenile," Jud said with a significant look toward Paulo. "You and your fiancée are testing my patience." His pole jerked and then the line unfurled quickly with a high pitched whine. "Hey, I've got one!"

Almost immediately, Paulo's pole did the same thing. "I have one and it is bigger than yours."

"How can you tell?" Lily backed away.

"A true fisherman knows." Paulo put a hand on his reel, putting a halt to the spinning.

Jud followed his lead.

"Is it possible you've both caught the same fish?" Lily wondered out loud, earning disparaging glances from the fishermen.

The yacht lurched forward, as if someone had stepped on the gas. The three of them struggled to keep from losing their footing. Paulo bent over the rail, nearly losing his fishing pole.

There was only one reason Lily could think of for the sudden acceleration. "Grandma Dotty!"

Social media disaster forgotten, Lily ran for the stairs.

The yacht careened to the right, nearly sending Lily to her knees. She grabbed onto the stair rail just as the boat surged forward and tilted to the left.

"Grandma Dotty!" Lily scrambled up two flights of stairs, raced into the dining room, and burst through the door into the control bridge where her grandmother had a death-grip on the controls. "Stop."

"That's not fair. I've barely begun." For all her petite stature, Grandma Dotty had wiry strength when she wanted something. And she wanted to steer.

"Stop, Grandma. Or I'll call Dad and tell him to pick you up in Charleston."

Pouting, Grandma Dotty released the controls. Her short silver hair glinted in the sunlight as brightly as the glint in her eyes. "I would have done fine if Captain Stubing here had just handed over the helm."

"No means no." The captain was a middle-aged gentleman. Like his crew, he wore white slacks and a blue polo shirt with the yacht's name and logo stitched on the breast. Unlike his crew, he wasn't giving in to Grandma Dotty's demands. "No more visits to the bridge. No more touching the controls."

"Well, I never." Grandma Dotty huffed. "I tried one time and you've already judged me wanting. All I need is another chance to prove my skill." She moved closer to the controls.

Lily lunged forward, grabbing onto her grandmother's thin arm.

The captain shook his finger. "No means no."

Lily supposed he could have dropped harsher judgment on them. "Come on. The guys have fish on the line."

"Really?" Grandma Dotty was suitably distracted. She ran to the rear of the dining room and out onto the rear deck, looking down toward the boat garage. "That must have been two ginormous fish."

"What makes you say that?" Lily wasn't as quick to join her.

"Because they got pulled into the drink." Grandma Dotty pointed out toward the wake behind them.

In the distance, two pairs of arms waved like mad. Lily could just make out one shaved head and one dark brown one. "Man overboard!" Lily practically flew toward the bridge, opening the door to shout it again, "Man overboard!"

"Men," Grandma Dotty corrected, waltzing past Lily and toward the controls. "*Men* overboard. We need to turn about."

The captain extended his arm to stop her while simultaneously reaching for the speaker. "Man overboard. Launch the skiff." He dropped the mic and grabbed Grandma Dotty by the shoulders. "Thank you, ma'am. We know who to call if we need backup." He turned her around to face the door.

"I guess no really means no," Grandma Dotty said, shoulders slumping in disappointment.

8

"My fish was big-big-bigger." Paulo's teeth chattered as he made the claim in the rescue skiff's bow. The bruise on his forehead was darkening and the size of a golf ball.

Jud scoffed and wrapped the blanket he'd been given tighter around his shoulders. He was cold, but not so cold that he couldn't snap back. "It doesn't matter whose fish was bigger. Your fiancée is a bully and all deals are off. When we get back, I'm telling her you speak English."

"You are just mad be-be-because your cell phone is wet." Paulo shivered. "My phone was swallowed by a b-b-b-big fish. The biggest fish. My fish."

Jud rolled his eyes. "The one you would have caught if we hadn't been catapulted off the yacht?"

"Yes. I blame you. You grabbed onto me."

Jud shook his head. "I was trying to save you from falling overboard. Remember that I have lightning fast reflexes. I rescue people for a living."

"On TV." The skiff driver laughed.

Jud and Paulo turned to look at him. The skiff driver was

the porter who'd helped with the luggage and served them their meals.

"Problem?" Jud asked in an icy voice.

"No, sir." And to prove it, he smiled.

"Eek!" Paulo drew back.

"Oh, my God." Jud covered his mouth and pointed at the younger man. "Your teeth." They were red.

The skiff driver stopped smiling. "It was the beets. Every time Mrs. Summer turned down an egg salad sandwich, the chef went ballistic. When she sent this one back, I ate it. Only now, everyone, including the chef, knows I did."

"Tough break, man. All she wanted was plain egg salad. Speaking of wants, I'll need a bag of rice to stick my phone into when we get back on board." Jud turned his attention toward the yacht. "Why didn't the yacht slow down or turn around?"

"We have a schedule to keep," the driver said. "And the captain is upset about Mrs. Summer trying to take over the boat controls."

"The love of my life nearly drowned." Rachel paced the boat garage. "Twice in one day!" She glared at Lily, who had a feeling that Rachel wanted to blame her.

"That's unlucky," Grandma Dotty said matter-of-factly. "Maybe you shouldn't travel by sea."

Rachel crossed her arms over her chest. Her red hair undulated in the breeze over one shoulder. "I won't rest until Paulo is in my arms again."

Marta put a consoling arm around Rachel's shoulders. "See? They're in the skiff, just a few more minutes away."

"I want him now." Rachel thrust Marta's arm off and went to stand at the safety rail.

"You shouldn't treat people like that." Grandma Dotty went to put her arm around Marta. "We're all worried."

"Yes, but only one of us is responsible for nearly drowning two men." Rachel waved to the skiff.

"Yes, your captain is to blame," Grandma Dotty said with complete conviction.

Anger flashed in Rachel's eyes.

"We'll let you wait in peace." Lily hustled Grandma Dotty away.

"Where are we going?" Grandma Dotty asked. "To call family? Have you looked at your phone lately? Your sisters are texting me non-stop. You know I'm not a good texter."

"I know. I'm ignoring them." Lily led her grandmother toward the salon.

"You need to answer."

"I did. I told them we were fine." It was the equivalent of no comment.

Behind her, Grandma Dotty scoffed. "You know they don't believe you. Violet is especially concerned."

"Do you believe me?" Lily stopped in the hallway and looked at her grandmother's sweet face.

She reached out to smooth Lily's curls over her shoulder. "You never back down from a fight, which is what makes you so good in public service fighting for the underdog. But whether you're fine... That's not for me to judge. It's just that you never told anyone what happened that night after Rachel abandoned you and now I think whatever it was...it should be out in the open."

"I'm fine," Lily insisted, turning down the short corridor to the salon. "And what Violet and the rest don't realize is that I have to do this on my own."

"Alone?" Her grandmother tsked. "Maybe in your fight with Rachel. But what about your past? And what about Jud? I can tell you're falling for him. You need your sisters and the Kissing Test."

"I don't." Lily turned and hurried down the hall. "I enjoy Jud's company. But I'm smart enough to realize I'm not his type. And since he isn't interested in a relationship, there's no Kissing Test needed."

Grandma Dotty harumphed. "For a woman who fights for everyone else, you're very quick to abandon a battle for a man's heart."

"A good general chooses battles they have a chance to win." Lily opened the door to the salon. "We're on a secret mission. We're borrowing a dress for dinner tonight."

"Both of us?"

"Yes." That hadn't been Lily's plan. But if it made her grandmother happy...

"I don't know, dear." Grandma Dotty quirked her white brows. "Those dresses of Rachel's aren't your style. They're too revealing. Why don't you borrow an outfit from me?"

Lily struggled not to laugh. Her grandmother meant well, after all. "That's not what this is about." She was about to say that she wanted to beat Rachel at her own game–wear a dress better than Rachel ever could, but the salon door opened.

"What are you doing in here?" It was Marta, looking like she'd caught trespassers.

"Playing dress up for dinner?" Lily tried to smile. "It seems a shame that you chose all these outfits and Rachel won't even wear them. I felt so fabulous last night after your make-over. I wanted to recreate the magic."

Marta gave both Summer women an assessing look.

"But it's great that you're here. You can help us with our

hair and make-up." Lily tried to project her most innocent smile. "As you can see, we need the help of an experienced stylist."

"Maybe just a professional hair fluff for me." Grandma Dotty's lips pulled to one side. "I think I'll stick with the clothes I brought. Most of Rachel's dresses have more room on the topside."

"Not the Angelina Jolie dress." Lily reached in the closet for the strapless black dress they'd rejected for their brides-maid duties.

"But...the wind on this boat..." Grandma Dotty's eyes widened. "Do you have black panties? With a slit that high, you're going to need black panties."

Lily shook her head, realizing that it wasn't just her work wardrobe that had become staid and stogey, it was also her underwear drawer.

"Never fear." Grandma Dotty raised her finger to the air. "I have a package of new underwear in my suitcase."

Undoubtedly, they were granny-panty style, but Lily supposed they'd at least provide full coverage in case of an unfortunate wind gust.

"I have appropriate undergarments in the drawer over there," Marta said with less starch than usual. "Sit in the chair and let's do something more formal with your hair."

Grandma Dotty went to dig through the drawer.

"Thank you." Lily hurried to plop into the stylist chair. "It's really kind of you to spend time with me. I hope Rachel won't mind."

"The bride is otherwise occupied." Marta assembled a collection of hair clips and combs. "Perhaps tomorrow you can wear some of the Stella McCartney collection. I was looking forward to seeing Rachel wear the floral pieces."

"Of course. I'd love to." Anything to win Marta over to her side.

"Marta, I think you've got your drawers mixed up." Grandma Dotty held up a pair of black panties made of sheer lace. "These are wedding night pieces. Lily might just as well go commando."

No one said anything for a moment.

And then Grandma Dotty added in a subdued whisper, "Forget I said that last part."

"Did you tell Rachel to lay off Lily?" Jud ordered a whiskey neat from the bartender. He'd seen Paulo at the lounge bar as he climbed the stairs to the dining room. When the big man didn't answer, Jud grabbed hold of his arm. "Did you?"

"But of course," Paulo whispered unconvincingly with a glance toward one of the chandelier cameras.

"Things had better change, Paulo. I'm warning you."

Dotty came up the stairs. She was wearing a floor length mauve dress. Her short silver hair had been teased into some semblance of order. "Are you coming to dinner, boys?"

"Yes," Jud said obediently. He poked Paulo.

"*Si*." Paulo headed for the stairs.

"It's going to be a glorious sunset." Dotty climbed the stairs with a slow but steady pace. "If you were looking for a big, romantic moment. Tonight's the night."

Jud didn't say anything. He hoped to spend time with Lily tonight, but not when in full view of Rachel and her cameras. If Lily wanted privacy, he'd provide it.

Dotty reached the dining room landing. She went to stand at the door separating the dining room from the bridge, crossing her arms and staring at the crew.

The captain came to the other side of the glass door, nodded to acknowledge Dotty, and then shut the drapes between the two rooms.

"That man." Dotty flounced around. "I think he blames me for you two falling overboard."

And rightly so.

Paulo hugged Dotty. "I forgive you."

"Forgive?" Dotty huffed, breaking free of the big man's embrace. "What's to forgive?"

Jud wisely kept silent.

Abe ascended the stairs, looking worn out. Even his spiky hair drooped. "Rachel's determined to go through with this wedding even though her agent is now telling her not to. Something about over-exposure." Abe was winded. He leaned on a chair back. "Why did I bring you along, Hambly? Nothing's happening."

"Abe, it's clear you need moral support." Dotty hugged him, patting his back as she added, "You should have offered a bonus to get things done in less than five days."

Abe disengaged himself and called for wine.

Rachel entered the dining room in a black pantsuit with a plunging neckline. Marta followed her in, silently moving to her place at the table but keeping her gaze on the staircase instead of on her mistress.

Paulo scurried to Rachel's side, showering her with kisses, murmuring in Portuguese, and making Jud want to slug him.

"Where's Lily?" Rachel gave Paulo a gentle push and stalked to her seat at the head of the table. "I hope Lily wasn't offended by my little post earlier. My social media is all about my brand, which is fashion."

"And backstabbing, which is cliché." Dotty was leaning over the stair rail, oblivious to Rachel's sharp intake of breath. She straightened. "Lily's almost here." She passed Jud on the way to her seat, grinning as if the captain's snub had been forgotten. "Don't get me wrong, Rachel dear. Every show must have its villain. It's just that this isn't a show. It's real life. And sometimes in real life, villains get their come-uppance." The way Dotty spoke–gleeful anticipation in her tone–it was as if Lily was about to enter the ring for a throw down contest between good and evil.

Adding to the impression, Marta leaned forward.

"Did I miss something?" Abe scanned the room.

Jud moved to the stairwell just as Lily rounded its curving steps beneath him.

Her hair was pinned in a sophisticated style around her head. Her make-up was brighter than usual–heavy black lined her eyes, false eyelashes fluttered gracefully against her cheeks, ruby red lips curved in a confident smile when she saw him. And her dress...

It was black and strapless. And with each step of her right leg, the front floor-length skirt parted nearly to the top of her thigh.

Jud couldn't move. He'd admitted there was chemistry between them. But this...Lily Summer wasn't boring or Mary Poppins. He wanted to date her. He wanted to date her for real. He had since the hot tub? No. Since their first kiss. Not even. It had been since the moment she'd slid her glasses on at the hotel and had fixed him with a look that said she saw right through him.

"Way to bring it, dear." Dotty blew an air kiss to her granddaughter when Lily reached the landing. And then she opened a flip phone and snapped a photo.

"I hope you didn't hold up dinner on my account." Lily signaled to the porter that they were ready to be served, a job usually executed by Rachel.

Jud and Paulo hastened to pull out Lily's chair.

"Paulo," Rachel sharply called her fiancé to heel. And when Lily was seated, Rachel looked at Lily and said, "Touché."

"Aren't you supposed to dress up on a cruise?" Lily laughed, a completely fake sound but exciting to Jud, nonetheless. "As you pointed out yesterday, I don't do it near enough." Lily glanced across the table, flashing a grateful smile. "Thanks for helping me with my hair and make-up, Marta."

"My pleasure." And Marta did look as if it had given her joy, despite Rachel's deep frown.

"How kind of you, Marta." Rachel's gaze narrowed in, targeting her minion.

Paulo tsked and drew Rachel closer for a kiss.

Jud hoped Rachel's discomfort and Lily's stunning appearance had been captured on camera. He found Lily's cold hand beneath the table and gave it a squeeze. "You look exquisite, like a classic Hollywood beauty."

"A femme fatale," Dotty murmured, causing Rachel's expression to turn thunderous.

The first course was brought in–Cajun shrimp with cucumber salsa. Jud sighed as he looked at his two shrimp. Two. Another night of food like this and he was raiding the kitchen.

"Who wants mine?" Dotty lifted her plate. "Shrimp gives me the toots."

Paulo's hand shot over the table to claim hers before Jud could.

"How goes the wedding planning, Rachel?" Lily's façade was cool, seemingly ignoring the tension Rachel radiated. But her hand wasn't warming in Jud's grip.

Rachel sipped her wine before answering. "We chose

flowers and champagne today. My bouquet is going to be made of lilies and white roses. Last time around, I made a mistake with everything. This time, everything is going to be perfect, including my groom."

"You can have a perfect ceremony next year," Abe muttered. "A true test of love is time."

Rachel sniffed but said nothing.

Paulo had inhaled his two shrimp and Dotty's two shrimp. He eyed Rachel's untouched shrimp, beaming at his intended, who handed him her plate.

Jud stared at his empty plate, and then dejectedly at Lily's.

"What else needs to be done?" Lily asked cheerfully, making him admire her spunk. "Maybe I can help."

"We need to select wedding bands." Rachel paused to admire her ring. "No simple band for my man. We have an appointment tomorrow morning in Charleston with an exclusive jeweler. On Friday, our minister arrives in Miami from Portugal. And then we'll have our beautiful moment and officially begin our lives together, like an open book."

"Have you been reading this book?" Dotty took a thin breadstick from a carafe on the table and crunched into it. "Or does the reading start after the ceremony?"

Lily looked worriedly at her grandmother.

Jud cleared his throat. "What about Abe and Paulo's family? And other guests you want to share this moment with?"

Rachel laughed, but there was a hollow sound to it. "Surely, you know. My social circle, including my show cast-mates, have decided to stay away this time. My father believes we're rushing things. He's not supportive at all." Her gaze drifted toward the window and the yacht's wake. After a moment, she added, "That's why you're here. We settled on a compromise. Guests Daddy *approved* of. Guests I could tolerate sharing my special moment with."

Tolerate? Uh-oh.

Lily, Dotty and Jud exchanged surprised glances that turned into wary ones. Like him, they were probably thinking: *This didn't bode well for Paulo making Rachel leave Lily alone.*

"I think your father supports you." Lily was the first to overcome her shock.

"Abe didn't want you to be alone," Judd added his two cents.

"Even if you're having a disagreement, he's still family." Dotty's eyes had teared up. "My son and I argue all the time. But he's still my son and worthy of my love."

"I can speak for myself." Abe got to his feet. "I love my daughter. But no one should give their child everything they ever ask for. It blurs their perspective. And for this, I'm sorry." He picked up his plate and left them.

"Please don't pity me. I'm turning all this into lemonade." Rachel's expression softened as she gazed toward the stairs. "My father made a promise to my mother before she died, a vow to take care of me. He can't see that my last marriage was a mistake or that what Paulo and I have is the deeper kind of love he and my mother had. Michael used me to cement a contract with my father. He didn't love me so much as the influence I had with my father. But Paulo..." Rachel touched Paulo's cheek. "We're soulmates. We made a connection without words. Although I am helping him renegotiate his contract with the Badgers, I know he'd never use me for my business connections."

The groom's smile seemed grim.

❧

"Turning my grandmother's hot tub performance request down tonight was the right thing to do." Lily reclined in a lounger, nestled beneath a blanket and in Jud's arms.

She'd changed out of her stunning evening gown and agreed to meet Jud in the boat garage, which was the only place not fitted with hidden cameras. Not to mention that the rushing water would make it hard for anyone to record their conversation. She'd been grateful for Jud's suggestion since she feared photographs of herself coming out of Jud's cabin if they'd talked there.

They were still an hour from arriving in Charleston. The air was growing warmer the farther south they traveled, but it was still chilly. Jud's body radiated welcome heat as they stared up at the stars.

"I admit," he told her. "I was worried about Rachel using clips of our hot tub singing. I'd rather not become a social media meme."

"Like me?" Lily tensed. "I don't think you're a target. She respects you and loves you a little bit, too." Lily couldn't keep the bitterness from her tone. She was becoming proprietary where Jud was concerned. "And tomorrow when we break up, she'll have her shot at you." Lily snuggled deeper in his embrace, blaming it on the cold when in reality, she didn't want the intimate moments with Jud to end. "How do you want to do it?"

Jud drew back, staring at her with raised brows.

"Oh, word choice. You know what I mean." Lily's cheeks heated anyway.

"I do. And I'd never pressure you to do something you aren't ready for."

Lily shoved her glasses into her hair and buried her face against his chest.

He lifted her chin and lowered her glasses ever-so-gently

until his face came into focus. "Studying character is an actor's job. Something happened to you after Rachel left you in that pop-up club. Something that makes you careful about the clothes you wear and the men you date. You can tell me. I'm here to listen."

"Why do you want to know?" Lily sounded meak and wary. But that's what life had made her.

"Because I want to know who you are. Not the person you project to the world, but the strong woman beneath the layers, the one with vulnerability in her eyes."

"Oh."

His arms came around her, drawing Lily more completely into the shelter of his embrace. "I'll wait."

Lily was certain that he would. She drew in a shaky breath. "I wanted to cry when she left. I was supposed to be the one protecting her, but then I had no one to protect, no one to be brave for." No twin to do both.

"Of course, you'd be afraid. You were seventeen, alone in a cage with men disrespecting you." He made it sound so simple.

He understood. Lily couldn't bring herself to speak. She could only nod.

"When did it get worse?" His question was as patient and comforting as his embrace.

The words she'd never spoken tumbled out. "When someone opened my door." Bodies, hands, hot breath and lewd suggestions. "I was dragged out and trapped in the crowd." The lights had been pulsing in time to the music. It was impossible to make out faces, to humanize anyone touching her. "They ripped off my blouse." The fabric, their nails. She had scratches all over her skin. "They would have torn me–"

Jud pressed her closer still, mangling her glasses. Not that she cared.

"–but the police showed up." Not that Rachel had called them. They were there on a drug raid. She'd collapsed as the party-goers had run out the back.

"I want to beat the crap out of every one of them," Jud whispered gruffly.

"That's what the cop who took me home said, too." Lily managed to work her head free and smile up at him. "They all scattered. It was so dark...I couldn't have identified anyone..."

Jud stroked her hair. "There was no one to press charges against? No slimeball to face in court?"

She shook her head.

"No closure," Jud murmured.

She shook her head again.

"And little progress forward," he said softly. "No therapy? No support groups?"

"I have four sisters. I've never been the girl who over-shares. I'm okay."

"You're more than okay." He surprised her by agreeing. "You are mighty fine. Mighty fine." He traced her cheek with his finger. "And I'm honored that you shared your story with me."

Lily blinked back unexpected tears. "Thank you for listening."

They stared at each other in silence.

Lily forced out a laugh. "I'm not much good at deep, soul-searching stares that come before deep, soul-searching kisses."

"Don't knock anything soul-searching. It's rare to find another soul I want to learn more about."

His words stole her breath. At least, until she remembered it was a line from one of his films. "I remember that movie. *Sentimental at Sunset.* Smooth line, Mr. Hambly."

"It worked though, didn't it?" His smile was a thing of beauty. It chased all the ugly memories back into their box. It helped that he kissed her.

"Is it midnight? It feels like midnight," Lily murmured. "It feels like my time with the prince is coming to a close."

"The fake dating part," he allowed.

She didn't want to argue about what wasn't going to happen when they got off this yacht. "How do you want to break up?"

"Can't we throw Paulo under the bus first? You heard Rachel tonight. She thinks their relationship is an open book. Knowing Paulo has understood her all this time might make her cancel the wedding."

Lily opened her mouth to argue, but instead found herself saying, "Are we an open book?"

Jud's arms loosened around her.

"I mean…" Lily hurried to explain. "Paulo said Rachel had recorded your conversation with your agent. Is there something I need to know?" Something that might make her regret sharing her past? She held her breath, hoping Jud would ease her mind.

"We argued about my image and my career trajectory," Jud admitted slowly. "Darian doesn't support my move to directing, mostly because I could make more money for both of us in the immediate future by committing to Titanium Talon for another three seasons. And I feel…I feel caught in the middle. Talon is more than just a superhero. He's flawed and dealing with a less than pleasant past he needs to resolve." Jud kissed Lily's nose. "But my dad… Man, he wants me to move on. It makes me wonder…"

"Don't doubt your talent as an actor. You're brilliant."

Lily lay her palm on his cheek. "An academy award nominated actor. You're not a hack."

"My father doesn't respect the superhero genre."

"Grandma Dotty would say you should always follow your heart. And it sounds like you have a love for playing Talon."

"Darian would say I should always build my bank account." Jud's fingers tangled in her hair, brushing up her nape. "But he's pulling for Talon, too. If I just didn't have this nagging feeling, like I'm missing an opportunity that's right in front of me." He stared into Lily's eyes.

She waited for his kiss, but it didn't come. "It's hard, isn't it? Figuring out what to do with your life, for the rest of your life?"

His fingers stilled. "Adulting, you mean?"

"Yes." Why wasn't he kissing her? After hearing her past, was he thinking he should dole out kisses sparingly? "Increasingly, I feel like I'm at a crossroads, like that heroine in the movie you want to direct. I know deep in my heart that I want to help others, but I'm just not sure that politics is the best place to do that." Not to mention there was a lot of repression Rachel and Jud had recently made her aware of.

Jud's hand cradled the back of her head, keeping her focus on him. "Instead of becoming the first woman mayor of New York City, you could start your own charity."

Because she wanted more touch, more connection, Lily ran her hand lightly up his arm, into her hair, linking her fingers with his. "Wouldn't I be a cliché then? An heiress always raising money for her personal charity?"

"Who cares what others think if it brings you joy?" He drew their joined hands down until they rested between their hearts.

"And we're back to following my heart." But not his. Lily realized he'd deftly swung the subject away from himself to her, and she'd let him, afraid that whatever he wasn't sharing would drive a wedge between them.

"It's late and we haven't finalized our plan to force Rachel's hand." Jud's voice was deep, rich and soothing. If they'd been anywhere else, she could almost believe she could fall asleep in his arms.

That was a first.

"Tomorrow at dinner," Jud was saying. "I'll accuse you of having feelings for Paulo. That will upset both Rachel and me. And then you'll storm out." The timbre of his words roughened. "Jealousy is a powerful emotion. My parents only fight when they're jealous."

Lily sighed. She knew jealousy too well. "My mother used to be resentful of my father's mistresses, and with good reason. Now she just self-medicates and pretends to be happy, which makes it easier for my father to be emotionally unavailable." Lily hated that selfish part of her father. "I often wonder how their marriage would have been if Mom had a fulfilling life or career before she'd married. Now, she has nothing of her own to keep her occupied or fulfilled. Their relationship is part of the reason I work so hard at my job and my future, more so than my ability to open up in a relationship. I want a place in the scheme of things before I commit to someone. And that man needs to be worthy of my trust. We need to be each other's open book." She hadn't meant to say so much, to reveal so much.

It must be the gentle motion of the boat. Or the shared secret mission they were on. Or the way the stars glimmered above them. Or a dozen things she loved about Jud and a dozen more she expected to find.

Things I love about Jud...

I could love Jud.

She was more than half in love with him already.

"You want truths?" Jud's arms tightened around her. "We may be breaking up tomorrow night, but I'm serious about taking you to dinner this weekend."

"I don't know."

Jud drew back, staring at her. "Explain."

"I'm comfortable with this fake relationship because I know there's no pressure for more than kisses."

"I told you I'm a patient man. You can trust me. Say yes, Lily. Say yes to weekend dinners with me."

Lily nodded, because Jud seemed to expect her to.

But increasingly, she felt he was hiding something in that conversation Rachel had caught on camera. Increasingly, she felt as if her heart was going to break tomorrow night.

For real.

9

"Ma'ams." Someone knocked on Lily's door far too early in the morning. "There's someone here to see you."

"If it's Abe, tell him to make a lunch appointment." Grandma Dotty rolled over and pulled the covers over her head. "And bring an egg salad sandwich."

"Who is it?" Lily put on her glasses, pulled on a bathrobe and went to the door.

The porter pointed to the porthole. "You can see them from your window. We're under strict orders not to let anyone else on board. Ms. Cohen and her fiancé have already disembarked."

Lily thanked him, closed the door, and climbed on her bed to look out the porthole. She gasped. "Time to rise and shine, Grandma Dotty. My sisters are here." Without waiting for an answer, Lily hurried to get dressed and ready to face her well-meaning, meddling sisters. She wore the flowery Stella McCartney pants Marta had loaned her and a flowing blue blouse.

Jud met them in the hallway. He wore a forest green polo

and khaki shorts. "I heard you have visitors. Let's get out of here for the day."

Our last day.

There would be no dates this weekend. Lily needed honesty in a man and she couldn't shake the feeling that Jud wasn't telling her something.

"Jud, dear, I..." Grandma Dotty seemed to be choosing her words carefully, for once. "Are you sure you want to accompany us? Some men find Lily's sisters to be a...a handful."

Lily shrugged. "It's his funeral." They'd submit him to the Kissing Test, for sure. And even though Lily wanted to believe he'd pass, it might be better if he didn't.

"Now I'm nervous." Jud tried to make light of it. "Do your sisters have superpowers?"

"Something like that," Lily agreed. She led them to the stairwell, up a floor and then down the gang plank to the dock.

Wisps of fog still clung to the water and shrubbery on the shoreline, but it promised to be a nice sunny day. The marina was full of yachts and people disembarking, heading toward shore.

"It's about time." Violet looked tired, her red blouse was as wilted as her hair. She enfolded Lily into her arms. "My twin spidey sense was doing double-time yesterday after that post Rachel made. Your hair looks marvelous." She stepped back to take her in. "And those trousers are fantastic. They make you look so happy."

"Looks can be deceiving," Lily murmured, causing Violet's eyebrows to skyrocket.

"We took the red-eye." Aubrey was next in line for a hug, easing Violet out of the way. She wore a blue polka dot dress over a pair of tights and black booties. She nodded toward Jud. "Is that the target?"

"There's nothing here to target," Lily told her, moving on to hug her youngest sister Maggie, who wore a black T-shirt, black jeans, and work boots.

"I hope you're wrong," Maggie said in a sour voice. "I lost a night of sleep because of you. I can't sleep on planes."

"Where's Kitty?" Lily asked before realizing the topic of their older sister was still taboo with Maggie.

"Kitty is interviewing at a hospital near Beck's horse breeding farm," Grandma Dotty said plainly, as if not remembering that Kitty had contributed to Maggie being stood up at the altar by Beck.

Pain flashed across Maggie's face.

"Never mind, honey," Lily said quickly. "I'm happy to see you–all of you–even if you lost sleep. But honestly, I've got everything under control." That was a whopper of a fib, but Lily was going to see this through. She'd signed a contract and she was determined that Rachel wouldn't get the best of her or see her break.

As usual, her sisters paid no attention to Lily's wishes. They glossed over greeting Grandma Dotty and pounced on Jud.

"How long have you known Lily?" Violet sidled up next to him.

"And what are your intentions?" Aubrey faced him head on.

Maggie shouldered her way into his face. "Forget all that and tell me if you knew about that steamy picture we saw of you two. Did you have anything to do with it being sold?"

Jud took it all in stride, slipping on his sunglasses and giving them a charming smile. "I met Lily Sunday. I didn't know the picture was being taken, obviously. Neither one of us did. We've been paired on this trip because we're the best man and maid of honor. And we just hit it off." He wove his way through their defensive line and put his arm around Lily's waist.

She allowed it, but only long enough to say, "We're not a thing. That kiss was just one of those impulsive moments that quickly fade into ancient history." She slipped free.

"Disagreeing," Jud said with the beginnings of a frown on his face. "We're going to dinner this weekend when we get back to New York."

"We're not." Lily headed toward land.

"We got here just in time," Violet announced.

Lily grimaced, but since she was ahead of the pack, she was certain no one saw. "Everyone looks like they could use a cup of coffee. Let's go have breakfast and then we'll find a place to shop." Shopping always lifted her sisters' spirits. And Charleston's King Street was filled with all kinds of shops.

"I don't watch your show," Maggie told Jud mulishly. "I don't watch any of those superhero shows or movies."

"She doesn't know what she's missing out on." Grandma Dotty gave a shout of laughter. "Imagine him in tights."

"They're actually compression armor," Jud said good-naturedly. "Every aspect of my suit has a purpose."

The Summer sisters dissolved into peals of laughter.

"What's so funny?" he demanded.

Lily turned at the dock's gate. "You're starting to believe your character's press."

"Yes, but it's a very well-developed character." Jud struck a superhero pose—legs widespread, fists on hips.

The Summer sisters swarmed past him, filling the air with their laughter.

There were several car services waiting in the marina's

parking lot, which said a lot about how exclusive the marina was. Somehow, Jud managed to claim a car and fill the back seat with himself, Lily, and Grandma Dotty. The girls grumbled and took the second car.

"I see now why I was warned." Jud half-turned, back to the car door. "This is the Summer Trial by Fire."

"The Kissing Test," Grandma Dotty nodded, earning an elbow nudge from Lily. "I wouldn't worry. If your feelings for Lily are true, you'll be fine. And tonight, when you see the dress Marta picked out for her...It will be magical, like Cinderella transformed for her prince."

Jud gave Lily a tender smile, to which she muttered, "And then everything goes back to the way it was." *I am such a downer today.*

"Life will never be the same." He tsked. "Cinderella will be rescued by Titanium Talon and they will live happily-ever-after."

Their driver gasped, staring at Jud in the rearview mirror. "It's you."

"It certainly is," Grandma Dotty said crisply. "Now, I know Jud told you to bring us to some swanky hotel for breakfast, but I want to go to a restaurant that serves egg salad sandwiches. And if you don't listen to me, I can be difficult."

"Whatever the lady wants." Jud drew Lily's hand into his, searching her face. "Because I have a feeling she's the only Summer in my corner. Am I right?"

Lily tried to pull her hand back. "You're making this into something it isn't, which will only make it worse with my sisters."

"Those sisters of yours want the same thing I do–to see you happy." Jud lifted her hand and pressed a kiss to her knuckles.

The warmth of his lips sent a trail of heat through Lily's arm, trying to melt her heart.

"I'm going to swoon. He's so romantic." Grandma Dotty squeezed Lily's arm.

"You're swooning because you haven't eaten enough on this trip." Lily managed to work her hand free. "I can't lie to my family. We're pretending. I'm nothing more to you than one of the weekly damsels in distress they feature on your show."

"Oh, no. He's in love with Aviator," Grandma Dotty said firmly. "He may be a playboy in real life, but he plays a smitten hero on TV." She frowned. "Did that come out right?"

"Yes," Lily said at the same time Jud said, "No."

"Listen to me, ladies. We're headed to one of the most popular tourist destinations in Charleston. We're going to be photographed." Jud captured Lily's hand once more. "My girlfriend and I are going to look like we're smitten with each other, because we are."

"Ooh. That's a good word for it." Grandma Dotty smiled and repeated, "Smitten."

Lily wanted to give in. She really did. "We both know I'm not the woman for you."

"Sure, you are." Jud touched a finger to Lily's nose. "And someday, I'll prove it to you."

"That day is sooner than you think." Grandma Dotty chuckled.

The driver took them to a quaint café that served both breakfast and lunch.

As much as Jud tried to sit next to Lily, her sisters

swarmed him like angry hornets, isolating him at the table.

Her identical twin Violet was the most intent on pinpointing Jud's feelings. "What do you like about Lily?"

"She makes me happy when we're together." Jud snagged Lily's gaze, thinking how content he felt when she was in his arms. "We don't even have to talk to–"

"She makes you happy when she doesn't talk?" Maggie was definitely the take-no-prisoners, glass-half-empty sister. "I'm happy when I deliver a foal or a calf. Don't need a man hanging around to make me happy."

The rest of the Summer clan heaved a collective sigh.

"What do you respect about Lily?" Aubrey hid her curiosity behind a pleasant smile.

Jud had never auditioned for the part of boyfriend before. What he needed was a character motivation speech, like the ones he made to directors when he was being considered for a role.

"I'm enjoying my plain egg salad sandwich." Dotty covered a burp behind her delicate hand. "It's so good that I may never leave."

Lily chuckled. "Whatever makes you happy."

And that statement, Jud realized, was the key to Lily. "Honestly? Lily is so down-to-earth that she grounds me. She cares more about others, and serving others, than she does about herself. He gave each Summer female a level glance. "She makes me think about my purpose here on earth when for years all I've been focused on is me and my career." He'd never uttered a truer statement.

And man, that went over well. The table went silent.

He was just congratulating himself when the Summers burst out laughing, even Lily.

"Those were heartfelt words." He let some of his irritation color his statement, rising to his feet. "I'm going to pay the bill." And get some much needed air.

"I care about others." Maggie had somehow leaped out of her seat to follow him, practically stepping on his heels. "And I have a big heart."

He glanced back at her, noting her forced smile and feral look in her eyes. It was good that she was a large animal veterinarian. She was no good as an actress. "Do you have a heart as big as Lily's? I noticed Lily apologized for bringing up your sister Kitty." He recalled Lily had mentioned to Abe that Kitty had stolen a sister's fiancé. Maggie's? That would explain her doldrums. "Do you still love Kitty?"

"I..." Maggie blanched. "That's none of your business. We can blow off the others and find an alley to make out."

The hostess was all ears as she rang up their tag.

Jud handed the hostess a wad of cash, including a generous tip and told her, "Do you see what celebrities have to put up with? For the record, I'm in a relationship with Maggie's sister. Now, run along Maggie and ask your sister's forgiveness for making a pass at me."

Maggie stomped off just as a group of college-age women entered the restaurant and squealed with excitement over meeting Titanium Talon.

They don't even remember my name.

Jud was a good sport anyway, posing for pictures before he escaped outside, slipping on his sunglasses. What was Maggie thinking propositioning him like that? It was then that he remembered what Dotty had said in the car about a Kissing Test. He might have laughed about it if he hadn't realized that Lily was letting this test play out. He wanted her to stand up and say she wanted to date him for real.

Right after she broke up with him tonight in front of Rachel.

He groaned.

Aubrey joined him next. "I'm star-struck, just like those college girls."

"I hope not." What he really needed right now was one of Lily's tender kisses. He glanced down at Aubrey. "Congratulations on your engagement." He'd seen her proposal at the animal rescue benefit the other night. And pointing that out seemed the quickest way to end this farce.

"Oh." Aubrey crossed her arms over her chest, looking insecure. "I hadn't realized you knew I was engaged. That makes this awkward."

"Doesn't it though?" He waved to someone across the street who called his name.

Aubrey raised a finger. "Hold that thought. Vi will explain everything." She darted toward the restaurant door.

"I'd rather hear Lily's explanation." And her apology, as long as it included a kiss or two.

"Sure," Aubrey said as she darted inside.

It took Violet a few minutes to reach him. She leaned her shoulder against the wall and looked at him through lowered lashes, as if she was trying to appear sultry. "You know that Lily and I are identical twins."

"And yet, you two are as different as salt and pepper." Jud gave her a sympathetic smile. "Why don't you tell me all about the Kissing Test? Clearly, you're all close to Lily. I admire that."

Violet considered him in silence for a moment, long enough for people to pass them on the sidewalk and snap his picture. "Has Lily told you anything about our parents?"

"Does your father's wandering eye count?"

Violet nodded. "When we were teenagers running wild about New York City, there came a point where we realized guys might be into us for the wrong reasons."

"Money? I have my own." And he was the only fourth generation Hambly. He'd inherit it all.

"Money," Violet said slowly, still searching his expression. "And guys are sometimes into girls for the physical benefits only. So, our sister Kitty developed the Kissing Test."

"Ah." Jud faced her, leaning his shoulder against the brick wall, too. "One Summer sister might easily replace another."

"Exactly." Violet nodded. "So, when we saw the picture of you kissing Lily–it was hot, I might add–without hearing a peep about you beforehand–"

"You assumed I was sweeping Lily off her feet for all the wrong reasons." The Summer sisters were a tight-knit bunch.

"You're smarter than your press." Violet didn't smile though. "Lily told me she's not going to be seeing you after tonight. She says she's unhappy about something, but she won't say what."

Jud swallowed back a burst of angry words refuting that statement. "We're in a complicated situation, but I assure you that I intend to date your sister long-term."

"Yeah. About that. Lily doesn't date anyone seriously." Violet backed toward the door. "We're taking Lily home with us tonight. We have a late flight out."

"You can't... She can't leave." There were too many reasons why, chief among them that Jud didn't want her to go.

Violet's brows went up. Way up.

Jud snagged Violet's arm. "I know what Lily went through. I'm willing to take things at her pace."

Violet's mouth formed a little "o."

"There's something real between us, an emotional

connection that Lily can't deny. Ask her." He wanted to come clean about the trip, but he'd signed a non-disclosure agreement with Abe. He couldn't explain and neither could Lily. "She's not going with you. She's staying with me."

Violet doubted it. She shook her head.

But Jud was certain. What he was feeling for Lily was real and could be love.

All he had to do to pursue the feeling was make sure their break-up was temporary.

10

"Marta, I bet the boat was quiet while we were all in Charleston today." Lily sat in Marta's stylist chair in the yacht's salon.

"And yet, the tension remains." Marta fiddled with Lily's hair on one side, drawing it away from her face and twisting the locks. She'd agreed to help Lily dress for dinner. "I can feel it in your shoulders. I heard you spent the day with your sisters."

"That's not why I'm tense." It was the approaching scene to be played in front of Rachel and the loss of Jud from her life.

"You'll feel so much better when you're all dressed up." Marta nodded toward the dress they'd agreed she'd wear. It was a scarlet bodycon dress that made Lily feel like a superhero.

The salon door opened, and Rachel entered, pausing to admire the dress. "What a lovely day. We found our wedding bands and spent the rest of the day at the spa getting massages. I feel marvelous." She looked it, too, in an unwrinkled white sundress.

Lily, on the other hand, looked wilted and windblown, like a woman who worked a regular job for a living and juggled too many things at once.

Rachel came to stand behind Lily, edging Marta away, and then smoothing her long red hair over one shoulder. "How are you feeling, Lily? It's been a big day for you, too. Did Jud pass your sisters' muster?"

"He passes my muster." Lily tried to look confident in Jud's affection, meeting Rachel's gaze in the mirror with a cool smile.

"He's too hot for you, girl." Rachel laid her hands on Lily's shoulders. "Haven't you ever wondered why he started dating you?"

"No." Lily's response carried no conviction.

Rachel reached in a pocket of her dress and produced her cell phone. "I have some video of Jud talking to his agent before we left New York. They spoke about you on the dock. Do you want to see the clip?"

"No." That, too, was a lie. Lily was desperate to know why Jud's conversation applied to her, why Paulo could use it to keep Jud from exposing Paulo's bi-lingual abilities to Rachel. But she didn't want the truth to come *from* Rachel. And maybe it was time to come clean about that. "Why are you doing this to me? The leaked photograph? The meme of us wearing the same dress? And now this video. Why do you want to hurt me?"

Rachel almost looked at a loss, blinking false eyelashes in apparent confusion. "Are you hurt?"

"Yes. Is that what you want to hear? Your actions hurt me. Your words and attitude hurt Marta and everyone who works on this boat. I'm sure everyone around you has felt your wrath, including your father. Why can't you realize that no one is out to get you?"

"I see myself completely differently." Rachel tossed her hair over her shoulder. "I'm trying to help you, but it's hard considering you make me feel like dirt."

"What? How?"

"Because you make me feel guilty for trying to save myself from those cages we were in. When I got home, I told Dad we had to find you. He insisted we call the police instead of going back. Guilt trip number one." Rachel's eyes glittered. "But the police told him they'd raided the pop-up party without finding a girl."

"They found me," Lily insisted, but for whatever reason, Rachel was having none of it.

"Guilt trip number two," she said. "Hoping you'd found your way home, Dad called your house, but your mother said you were fine and away visiting Kitty."

"That's what they told her when I ran away."

"Guilt trip number three." Rachel's eyes teared up. "I thought you'd been dead or kidnapped and sold into slavery."

There were tears in Lily's eyes, too. "I'm sorry. They were trying to protect me."

"I got shipped off to that jail-like boarding school. No phone. No internet." Rachel swiped at her nose. "You were my friend, Lily. Or at least, I thought you were. When I came home for Christmas and Dad finally let me have my phone, there was nothing from you. No text message. No missed call. No private message on social media. Nothing. And all I could think of was that you blamed me for what happened. For whatever happened."

"But..." So much had been assumed by both of them. "I thought you couldn't face me. I had no messages or phone calls either."

"No." Rachel swiped her hand through the air. "This isn't

about you. I came home and asked around about you. Everyone said you were fine. Still going out with Vi. You were fine and I wasn't. Everything worked out for you, but not me. I'm a reality star that everyone hates and you're this freaking paragon of virtue!" Her broken voice filled the room.

Lily felt the first stirrings of anger, like a chill, unexpected breeze across her arms. "I thought you said I was repressed."

"This isn't *your* narrative!" Rachel's voice cracked and she gasped for breath. "I carried this stupid guilt and you were fine. I thought you hated me and it ate me up inside. And then I realized that it wasn't on me, not all of it. You're to blame too. You could have told me running away was dangerous and wouldn't solve anything. You could have told me that dancing in a pop-up club was too great of a risk. You could have–"

"You're blaming me?" Lily was incredulous.

"Yes!" Rachel raged on, punching her arms out. "Do you know what it was like for me after Mom died? My dad was suffocating in his efforts to protect me. If he wasn't working some new business deal on the way to creating this global conglomerate of businesses, he was telling me what to wear, what to say, how to act, making a fool of me in front of my friends. In front of you!" Rachel jabbed a finger toward her. "The only way I ever felt in control was to be in control, to mesmerize all the men, to outwit and out-talk all the women. And to never, ever again allow someone to make me feel the way you did."

No wonder Rachel's so-called friends had turned down wedding invitations a second time. Rachel was just as out of touch with reality as Grandma Dotty. Only Rachel had fangs and minions.

Although Marta was slowly backing toward the door, most likely not wanting to be a part of this showdown.

And there was going to be a showdown. Lily had been bullied, tested, submitted to personal attacks and ridiculous accusations. Anger ran through her veins and balled her fingers into fists. She got out of the stylist chair and stood her ground. "According to you, everything bad that happened when we ran away was my fault."

"Yes." Rachel laid a hand over her chest as if ready to swear it could be nothing else. But then she paused, the way Grandma Dotty did when she thought a reality check was in order.

"You can blame me if it makes you feel better." Lily refused to believe it did. "But things weren't fine in the pop-up club after you left. Things got worse. Much worse. And I was lucky to make it home. But then, like you, I was grounded. After which, it was months before they allowed me cell phone privileges. And like you, I checked my messages." Lily held out her arms. "Nothing from Rachel."

Rachel's hand rose to cover her mouth.

"And now I'm here, at your father's request, trying to talk you into taking a breath and taking stock of what's happening in your life. And I'm realizing that you've been too quick to judge a lot of people. Yes, you." Lily shook her finger at Rachel the way Grandma Dotty often shook her finger at others. *I have been hanging around her too much.* "Yes, I dropped you cold, the same way you dumped me. And I probably should have been the bigger person and reached out to you, but I was hurting and healing from things that happened after you *abandoned* me. But unlike you, I didn't let things get twisted in my head until I accepted no responsibility for what happened. Geez, Rachel. We used to be friends. I used to think you were one of the happiest, funniest girls I knew. We used to recite lines from *The Hunger Games* and complete each other's sentences. What happened to us?"

Rachel blinked rapidly, gaze sweeping the floor. "You can't talk to me like that." Her words were little more than a whisper.

Lily made a snap decision. She marched over to Rachel. "I think what we went through gives me every right to talk to you like that." Lily hugged her, a quick catch-and-release. And then Lily moved toward the door, passing Marta, passing the red dress. She paused, hand on the knob, unwilling to flee before she tried one last time to reach the Rachel who used to be her friend. "I hope you find a happy place, Rachel." Lily opened the door.

"Don't go." Rachel's plea surprised Lily. It shouldn't have. It wasn't a plea. It was a trap. "I need to show you the video with Jud and Darian. I've got it all cued up to the important part. The wind sometimes interferes with the audio, but you'll get the idea."

"No." Lily held up a hand as she stepped into the hall. "Not interested."

"I'm going to play it anyway." Rachel fumbled with her phone. "You deserve to hear it."

Safe and mundane.

That's what Jud thought of her. That's what she'd heard on Rachel's video.

The only reason Jud had asked her out was because he wanted a fake girlfriend to help his image and make investors feel more comfortable buying into his film.

Someone no one in the media would be interested in. Someone he wouldn't be tempted to sleep with.

Lily wanted to be sick. Instead, she prepared for her final big scene in this Rachel-fueled drama.

Rachel, who thought she was protecting her former friend/former enemy/refound friend by playing that video.

With friends like Rachel, who needed enemies?

Lily stared at her reflection. Her brown hair had a bad case of the frizzes. Her plain, black-framed glasses seemed as mundane as her label. And her dress? Well, she hadn't gone with the red designer number. She'd put on the simple gray sheath she'd brought to wear to Rachel's wedding before she'd been recruited as the maid of honor.

"Tell me again what I do in my supporting role?" Grandma Dotty had changed into a long brown dress and an orange sweater.

Someone knocked on the door. "Room service."

"About that..." Lily went to answer the door. "I want you to sit this one out." Rachel was an emotional rollercoaster.

The porter stood in the hallway holding a plate with an egg salad sandwich. "Compliments of the chef."

Lily took the plate and put it on the small dresser beneath the television. She thanked the porter and closed the door. "I took the liberty of ordering in for you tonight. You know how high strung Rachel is." Lily was just as high strung and there was no telling how this dinner and break-up plan was going to go. "Two egg salad sandwiches in one day. That's lucky."

"But I'm part of your supersquad. We're on a secret mission." Grandma Dotty approached the plate. "It looks like a plain egg salad sandwich. How did you manage this?"

"I asked nicely." Actually, Lily had gone into the kitchen after Rachel's heartbreaking reveal, needing something to occupy her brain. Discovering the chef was still shopping in town, she'd made the sandwich herself and devised a time for delivery with the porter.

Grandma Dotty picked up the sandwich and took a bite. "It's quite good. Just like I make it at home."

Lily nodded. After all, her grandmother had taught her how to make egg salad.

There was another knock on the door. This time, it was Jud. Lily managed to smile at him, but just barely.

He looked handsome in his dark blue suit. If he was surprised that Lily hadn't gone the extra mile in her dress and appearance tonight, he didn't show it. His smile was as bright and charming as ever. "You ladies look ravishing. Are we ready?"

"I've been benched." Grandma Dotty plopped down on the bed. "But if I hear yelling, I'm going to come running."

Jud high-fived her. "Good to know you've got our backs. Shall we, Lily?" He stepped into the hallway and gestured toward the staircase.

Lily's gut clenched as she joined him. She didn't want to do this. From this point on, Lily was alone. Jud wasn't falling in love with her. He'd been using her to bolster his image, the same way Rachel was using her. Lily was one part angry, one part hurt, and one part numb.

"You look gorgeous," Jud said in a gruff voice, taking her hand and tucking it in the crook of his arm.

Lily didn't believe that for a second, but she held on to him all the same. There were memories to be made and lessons to be learned. But Lily knew that you had to survive the bad to know which were which.

"I mean it," Jud insisted. "You look gorgeous all the time. To me." He turned her at the stairwell, as he had a few times before. "I need a kiss to tide me over until this weekend. I'm taking you to dinner, remember? Saturday and Sunday."

Lily remained mute. But she couldn't kiss him. If she did, all the knots inside of her would come undone and she'd melt into a puddle at his feet. "A kiss for luck," Lily said instead. She pressed two of her fingers to her lips and then pressed them to his, bolting up the stairs instead of catching his reaction.

"Dinners this weekend though. And we can talk. You know I'm a good listener." She had to hand it to him. Jud was in tune with her safe, mundane moods, sensing her reluctance to commit.

Lily should have ascended the stairs in silence, calmly collecting herself for the emotional boxing ring she was about to enter. Instead, she said sharply, "We both know that your weekend dates won't happen."

Jud made a sound of frustration. "What's wrong? Talk to me."

She'd already said too much. Lily kept climbing, hurrying because she didn't want to argue with a man who'd lied to her all this time. When she reached the landing, she snapped, "I don't want to hear any more about it." It was the scripted line they'd planned on the car on the ride back from Charleston.

Lily held her head high as she crossed the room and took her place next to Paulo.

Jud sat next to Lily, radiating annoyance. Was that because she hadn't agreed to dinner this weekend? Or had the acting begun?

He was always acting with me.

Lily smiled at Rachel, although it felt as if she was baring fangs. Rachel had put on the red dress! *Grrr!* "Rachel, you told me you selected wedding rings, but you didn't say what kind of rings they were." How did actors do it? It was so hard to pretend to care.

"Platinum. Black diamonds. *Tres chic.*" Rachel ran a hand over Paulo's thigh. "I heard your sisters showed up. I bet Jud was no match for them."

"I was," Jud said crossly. "Now if it was Paulo facing the Summer sisters..."

Lily took the lob, giving Paulo a starry-eyed look. "He would have passed, too." She gave the groom's arm a proprietary squeeze.

Jud reached across her body, took her hand, and returned it to her lap. "You can give the man some breathing room. In fact, why don't you sit on the other side of the table? Next to Rachel. Go on." He gave her shoulder a gentle nudge.

"Jud, stop." Lily frowned at her hands in her lap, unable to look him directly in the eyes. "You're making something out of nothing." She forced herself to look at Rachel. "Where's Abe?"

"He had a business call. He told me not to hold dinner. And here comes the first course now." Rachel sat back to allow the porter to serve her. "Pancetta crisps with goat cheese and diced pear. I love a multi-course meal with these small servings. Just enough to tantalize your taste buds without weighing you down."

Jud scowled at his small plate.

Lily leaned toward Paulo and said in Spanish what she would have said to Jud in English before she'd learned what he really thought of her. "That can't be satisfying."

Jud. She ground her teeth. Of course, Jud was willing to take things slowly. He had no real interest in her. No spark of attraction. Everything was a lie, including those kisses.

Lily realized she was practically in Paulo's lap and had

lost her train of thought. "Look at that plate, Paulo," she told him in Spanish. "It's hardly enough to fill a man up."

Paulo chuckled, glancing at Rachel's plate but speaking to Lily in Portuguese, "If I am quick, I can convince Rachel to give me hers."

Lily forced out a laugh, handing Paulo her plate. "Here. Have mine."

Paulo pounced, practically swallowing her appetizer in one bite.

"Lily." Jud leaned in closer, but didn't lower his voice. "I would have eaten yours."

"Why are you feeding my fiancé?" Rachel frowned.

The porter set down a serving tray nearby and began to clear dishes.

"Lily pays your fiancé too much attention," Jud griped. His tone was sharp enough to cut Lily's feelings into bite-sized chunks, leaving small bits of fight and confidence for Lily to scrape off the floor.

Lily drank a generous amount of white wine while leaning against Paulo's shoulder. "I'm the only one here who speaks Paulo's native language. Of course, I'm going to go out of my way to make him feel at ease."

"That's Rachel's job." Jud was still in Lily's space, still radiating annoyance.

But Rachel was coming in a close second in the upset department. "Leave my man alone...*friend.*"

Lily growled. She'd never growled before.

The porter's grip on a small plate slipped. It clattered into another one.

Lily jumped.

Jud laid a hand on her thigh.

Safe and mundane.

Lily angrily brushed him off.

The porter began serving them chestnut fennel soup in those little fancy shot glasses the chef preferred.

"What is going on?" Paulo asked in Portuguese. "Why are you and Jud fighting?"

"Don't worry about it," she answered back in Spanish. *I'm just a girl who was made a fool of.*

"I am worried." Paulo laid a hand on Lily's shoulder.

Bingo!

Lily's gaze flew to Rachel's face.

"*Paulo,*" Rachel said in a voice that would command a puppy to obey. And then her dagger-filled gaze landed on Lily. "I see it now. You always sit next to what's mine. Whispering. Touching. Making passes." Rachel played right into Jud and Lily's hands, even though she knew they were here to stop her wedding.

Lily's stomach roiled with anger and mortification. She wished her part in this drama was over. She wanted to go home and mope in her bed for a week. But she also wanted to give everyone at the table a piece of her mind.

Grrr! She growled again.

Jud gave her a questioning stare.

"I was only making Paulo feel included." Lily took her wine and got out of her seat, coming around to relocate in the chair next to Rachel and across from Paulo, which would have been perfect if Jud had been as out of her line of sight as he was out of reach.

He tried to use me.

"Someone else can drink my soup." Lily had no stomach for food. And in the war between anger and mortification, anger was winning out.

"I don't think you're as innocent as you claim," Rachel said slowly. "This is payback for the argument we had earlier."

"What argument?" Jud's gaze was piercing.

"Why is Paulo yours, Rachel?" Lily's anger was rising, building inside of her like a simmering volcano. "You don't love him. You want to possess him, like a toy."

"He likes being mine," Rachel said in a hard voice. Her cheeks were flushing redder than her hair. "Just like you enjoyed being Jud's. At least until I told you that you were just a convenient wallflower."

"What?" Jud jerked in his chair.

Lily kept her gaze on Paulo, so freaking hot with anger that she could barely keep still. "Who cares if Jud tried to use me to improve his image? You've done the same thing with all the guys you've been with, Rachel, including Paulo. It's just that he's easy to control since he doesn't understand a word you say."

"True that." Rachel nodded.

Understanding dawned in Paulo's eyes, followed by hurt.

Lily hadn't wanted to hurt anyone but the time for peace had long passed.

"Lily," Jud said in a quiet voice. A lying voice. "Lily, we need to talk."

Lily refused to look at him. She'd embarked on this trip with the goal of feeding the hungry and sheltering the disadvantaged. To do that, she'd agreed to be heartless when it came to so-called love. As far as she was concerned, that meant the feelings she had toward Jud.

Lily turned toward Rachel. "There's just one flaw in your plan, *friend*."

"And what's that?" Everything about Rachel was red–her dress, her hair, her face. Anger didn't sit well on her.

Lily leaned forward. "You've become a cheater, Rachel. A liar. A woman who exploits the vulnerabilities of those closest to her instead of protecting them. But you're not the only despicable being in this room. Paulo lied to you. He speaks fluent English." Ignoring Rachel's sudden screech, Lily got to her feet as the porter came in with the salad course. Lily's gaze drifted toward Jud, which was stupid. It allowed every injustice from him she was trying to suppress rise up in her throat and demand she give it voice. "As for you, Judson Hambly, you can't bamboozle me." *Bamboozle*? Lily grimaced. Another of Grandma Dotty's words. "I'm not for sale or rent as your boring, fake girlfriend."

"I didn't…" Jud shot Rachel a dark look, but she was too busy slapping and poking Paulo's arm and accusing him of being a liar. "I did. But only at first. Before I got to know you. It was a stupid idea and I apologize."

"Too late," Lily snapped.

"Paulo, how could you lie to me?" Rachel's face was still beet red. She waved the porter away.

"Your first words to me? Speak to me in the language of love." Paulo's hands were circling the air, emphasizing every English word. "And then you kissed me and told all your friends that I was the perfect lover since I speak no English." Paulo's hands were moving as quickly as his mouth–up, down, around. "You did this."

"Oh, really." Rachel crossed her arms over her chest. "I am so done with you."

"Babe, we've got to talk." Jud used the lull in their argument to call to Lily softly.

"Don't *babe* me." Lily stalked around Rachel, pausing between the discordant bride and groom. "Everything on this boat is a sham. Rachel isn't the poor little rich girl who's misunderstood. Paulo isn't a master at the language of love. And Jud isn't the playboy actor who suddenly fell in love with a wallflower. I can't make any of you see the truth of how you hurt those who love you. The only thing I can do is make you question if you really love the person you say you do." That was a stretch since Jud had never told Lily he loved her. But it was time to apply the Kissing Test.

Lily bent and kissed the would-be groom on the lips. Not because Paulo was Rachel's fiancé, and it might drive the final stake into their wedding plans. Not because Lily wanted to make Jud jealous. But because they all needed to be shocked into questioning what love really meant to them.

"I resign as maid of honor." Lily straightened and stared straight into Jud's eyes. "And just so we're clear, Mr. Hambly, Mary Poppins isn't safe and mundane. She's magical and she rocks!" And then she left them.

Lily marched downstairs, packed her bag and her grand-mother's, and left the yacht, dragging Grandma Dotty with her.

If she had any luck, there'd be two seats left on that last flight to New York her sisters were on. She'd fallen in love with Jud in four days. Somehow, she knew it would take her a lot longer to forget him. But with any luck, she'd find those seats and forget that Judson Hambly had ever held her in his arms.

.

11

"The nerve." The words lacked Rachel's usual punch. She told the porter to cancel the rest of dinner.

For once, Jud wasn't hungry. "You should talk about nerve, Rachel. You recorded my conversations? All our conversations?"

"I had every right. You signed a waiver." Rachel stuck her nose in the air. "Why are you worried about that? Lily kissed my fiancé. Why didn't you stop her, Jud?"

"I would have liked to." He'd been sucker punched. Not only did Lily know the label he'd used to describe his ideal boost-my-image girlfriend, but she didn't believe his feelings for her were real. This trip was a nightmare. "Paulo didn't pass the Kissing Test," Jud added absently. "That means Paulo doesn't love you, not the way he should."

"What? What is this test?" Rachel turned on the more likely candidate to have halted that kiss–Paulo. "Why didn't you stop her, Paulo?" There was confusion on her brow and anger in her eyes.

Jud could relate to the jumble of emotions–shame because he'd hurt Lily, anger because she'd kissed another man, frustration because she'd never believed he'd wanted to date her in the first place. And the truth was that he hadn't at first, or at least, not consciously. But no matter what intentions had brought them together, Jud didn't want to lose her.

Paulo sat staring into the distance, looking the way Jud felt–as if something important had been ripped from his life and he wasn't sure how to get it back.

"Paulo, answer me." Rachel gave his arm a little shake.

Where was Dotty with her interrogation technique when Jud needed her. He channeled the old gal's bad Jimmy Cagney impression. "Why did you kiss her, man?" It was alarming to realize his fists were clenched. "You've told me this entire trip that you love Rachel."

"He told you that?" Rachel's tone softened. She rubbed the top of Paulo's shaved head as if he was a beloved dog. "Why didn't you tell me you speak English?"

"We are better off not arguing," Paulo said slowly, still not looking at Rachel.

Good for Rachel. If Paulo had looked, he'd have seen a calculating expression.

"I'll forgive you that kiss, *bae*, if you agree that I will always wear the pants in the family."

"That hardly seems like a good beginning to a marriage." Although at this point, Jud didn't care if they got married or not.

"There can only be one alpha in a marriage." Rachel cupped Paulo's face in both palms. "And it has to be me. Just look at Paulo. He's tall, sweet, and sexy. But he's just an athlete approaching the twilight of his career. I'm the real wage earner. There are years of wage-earning ahead of me."

Paulo subtly rolled his shoulders back.

"Every marriage has roles." Not that Jud had any experience in the matter other than playing the love interest in film and TV. "But you should treat each other as equals and with respect."

"I will spoil this man like no other." Rachel stroked over Paulo's ears with both hands, bringing her palms back to rest on his cheeks. "But that comes with a price. I negotiate all contracts. Paulo's agent is soft. I brokered a better deal with the Badgers, one that just landed on his agent's desk." She was talking to Jud not her fiancé. "I've told everyone that Paulo doesn't speak English. He can't utter another word of it now in public. I know what's best for us."

"This marriage has disaster written all over it," Jud said.

"I must speak my truth, like my friend, Lily." Paulo got to his feet, brushing Rachel's hands away. "Let me use small, simple words. I love you, but I am not stupid. I have pride. The wedding is off." He tromped off down the stairs.

Abe passed him as he entered the dining room. "I thought we were having dinner."

"The wedding is off," Jud said, not without some satisfaction.

"He left me?" Rachel's voice sounded childlike. She stood and went into her father's arms.

"It's okay, honey," Abe reassured her. "I had to ask your mother to marry me three times before she said yes. If he's your man, you'll work it out."

"If she was nicer, they could work it out quicker," Jud muttered, finding his feet. It was past time to go find Lily and beg her forgiveness.

"Don't leave me," Rachel said in a stronger voice, stepping away from Abe and crossing her arms over her chest. She faced Jud. "And then there were two."

Jud stumbled. "I'm not interested in being the last man standing on the Rachel Show."

"But you have to be." Rachel lunged for his arm, grabbing hold. "Do you know why the cameras are all over the yacht?"

Abe came to the table and drained Paulo's wine.

"Because you have issues?" Jud tried to extricate himself from her hold, but her grip on the arm of his suit jacket was like a vise.

"Because I'm editing content for a pilot, just for me. Agree to marry me in Paulo's place and I can re-edit the pilot." Her eyes glittered with the chill of winter. "Your stock will rise in Hollywood."

"As your boy toy? That is highly unlikely." Jud pinched her fingers from the fine wool of his jacket. "Do you even understand the plot of reality television? A show has to have someone real and relatable at its core." He'd studied story structure enough to know that reality TV was best when it had all the elements of scripted TV. "Relatable. That's not you."

Abe moved on to Rachel's glass.

"It could be you." She reached for Jud again.

He dodged back. "No chance in hell. I'm in love with Lily."

They both froze.

Did I just say that out loud?

Rachel started laughing.

"I fail to find the humor in this." Lily hated him. And rightly so.

"Do you honestly think Lily will believe anything you tell her now?" Rachel sank into the chair Paulo had vacated. "She won't. But I have your confession of love on film, which I will gladly give to you."

"For a price? Not a chance." Jud moved toward the stairwell. He was done with the Cohens.

"Let's go home, honey." Abe reached for the wine bottle on the buffet.

"*No!*" Rachel's voice was no longer calm and cold. Her voice was sharp, a painful cry for help. "My price for this cut of film is five million dollars."

Five...

Jud turned slowly back around. "You want me to pay you five million for a clip of me confessing my love for Lily? You really need to work on your people skills." But props to Rachel. She was evil and brilliant. She was mesmerizing to watch. "I just can't see you and Lily ever being friends."

"That's exactly what Lily told me, although in more words. But no." Rachel was folding Paulo's napkin slowly and with precision. "I'm not asking you for cash. Five million dollars is the exact amount of money my father promised you if you helped stop my wedding. I want you to tell him the deal is off."

"But..." Jud stopped himself from saying on camera that he'd fulfilled his end of the bargain.

"Rachel, a deal is a deal." Abe topped off a large glass of wine.

"Everyone is leaving me, Daddy." Rachel slumped in Paulo's chair. "All I have left is you. I'm going to protect you the way you've always protected me." She gave Jud a slow, considering look. "Dotty may not have all her marbles, but she knows what sells movie tickets. Your movie is a bad investment."

"We shook on the deal," Abe said wearily. "I can't renege."

"But he can back out." Rachel's stare pinned Jud in place. "It's like the Kissing Test, only with money. You have to prove how much you love Lily."

She was asking him to choose between Lily and a path

his family approved of. Even while everything was blowing up in her face, Rachel was pivoting, scrambling, refusing to give up. She wanted fame more than she wanted love. To an actor, she was a fascinating character. He didn't know if she was hooked on a chemical substance, a closet drinker, or had a health issue that made her pendulum swing at dizzying speed.

It was then that an idea formed. A stupid idea. Lily wouldn't approve. But it might help them all find peace and happiness.

He turned to face Rachel. "I have an alternative solution."

After taking the rest of the week off, Lily had spent Monday morning meeting with her staff. They filled her small office and discussed the repercussions of the days Lily had spent on the Cohen yacht.

Admission number 1: *Representative Lily Summer went on vacation with childhood friend Rachel Cohen.*

Admission number 2: *Representative Lily Summer met and briefly dated actor Judson Hambly. She regrets that a crew member felt the need to profit from a photograph of them together.*

Admission number 3: *Representative Lily Summer is no long seeing Judson Hambly.*

How Lily wished she could go back and rewrite the events of last week, starting with her reaction to Jud's card being handed to her by a waiter. She should have slipped on her glasses and read his note: *You have the most beautiful eyes. I'd like to get to know you better.*

She should have shown the card to Violet before

allowing Jud to escort her anywhere. Violet would have tested his sincerity right there and then. If that had been the case, Abe's offer to help Hot Meals and Shelter would have expired and she never would have set sail on his yacht.

Lily frowned, but only briefly because her staff all took note.

She waved their concerns away. "I'm fine. What it comes down to is this: *I'm human.* Thank you all for understanding." Lily looked at each of her four staff members in turn. "Next item on the agenda. Hot Meals and Shelter received a very large, generous donation today, one which will keep their doors open for at least another year." Turns out, the cost of keeping people fed and sheltered in her district was a broken heart.

Her team applauded. No one asked if Lily's sudden vacation coinciding with the donation to the food bank were related. But Lily knew that someone would.

She glanced at the next item on her list and swallowed. This was the hardest news to review. "We're supposed to begin discussing re-election plans, but after much soul-searching, I've decided I won't be running for re-election." One of the lessons she'd learned from her time with Rachel was that she needed to reclaim her identity. The one those men had stolen from her fifteen years ago. Today, she'd worn a fuzzy pink sweater over a white skirt that fell above her knees. Not exactly politician attire. At least, not a staid and mundane politician. She was tired of playing it safe.

There was a knock on the door.

"Who's that?" Nina asked. "We're all in here." She opened the door.

"Lily, I need your help." It was Grandma Dotty. She wore camel-colored slacks and a white turtleneck sweater beneath a white raincoat. She would have looked the height of matronly fashion, except her hair was still tinted silver and she wore bright yellow sneakers. "My birthday is coming up and I want the cast of *The Music Man* to perform."

The room was silent. No doubt, everyone was making the leap from the popular Broadway musical to one of its most popular stars in the past year–Judson Hambly.

"Hello?" Dotty repeated her request. "Did you hear me?"

Lily nodded, imagining she could hear her own heartbeat pounding out a warning.

"Hello, Nina. Hello, Zach. Hello, Tunda. Hello, Ayaliya." Grandma Dotty chuckled. "I feel like I've stepped into an episode of *Romper Room,* only I've forgotten my magic mirror."

Finally, Lily found her voice. "Doesn't Mom usually plan your birthday party?"

"Yes. But she and your father told me I couldn't have *The Music Man.*" Grandma Dotty tsked, came around Lily's desk and sat on the arm of her chair. "I'm old enough to have whatever I want. And besides, it's on my bucket list." She beamed at Lily's staff. "So, I've come to the office of my favorite politician to ask for help in the matter."

"No," Lily choked out.

"No?" Her grandmother's brow wrinkled. "As in, no you can't use your political power to help me? Or no, you, my granddaughter, won't help me?"

Lily waved her staff out the door, waiting until Nina closed it behind her to gently bring her grandmother to her feet. "You can't ask me to help you. Jud lied to me. I explained all this to you on the plane ride home." She stopped herself short of asking Grandma Dotty if she remembered.

Grandma Dotty folded her legs and sat down on the

floor next to Lily's chair. "That's it. You left me no choice but to stage a sit-in." And then she began to sing *Seventy Six Trombones*.

Lily closed her eyes and tried to slow her breathing. Her heart hurt whenever she thought about Jud. She wasn't up to seeing him again. Not yet. Maybe not ever.

"Seventy six trombones caught the morning sun," Grandma Dotty warbled.

Lily buzzed Nina at her desk. "I need you to draft a letter stating I'm not running for re-election." She had to repeat herself twice before Nina understood.

"There were over a thousand reeds..."

Lily pounded out an email on her laptop to Zach requesting he begin writing a speech about her stepping down at the end of her term.

"Clarinets of every size!"

Lily emailed Tunda asking her to swing by Hot Meals and Shelter since it was on her way home and congratulating them on the donation.

"Seventy six trombones hit the counterpoint."

Ayaliya poked her head in the door. "Sorry to bother you, but you need to proof our social media post about brownstone rezoning changes that are coming." She carried her laptop in and held it while Lily read the post.

"Run with it," Lily told Ayaliya.

"And they're marching still right today!" Grandma Dotty practically shouted the last line before sinking back against a filing cabinet. "I might need oxygen."

"Take slow, deep breaths." Lily rested her elbows on her knees. "I can't help you."

"You have to. That silly agent of Jud's won't take my calls." Her grandmother pouted. "How am I supposed to get in touch with him?"

Lily sat back in her chair. "I don't have his cell phone number. Contact him through social media."

"I thought of that." Grandma Dotty continued to pout. "I forgot my password. It's not like I'm asking you to call Jud. His snooty agent might accept your call."

Lily wasn't calling anyone. "You can reset your password. They'll send you a link to your email to do it."

"I forgot my email password, too." Her grandmother extended her hands, silently requesting help getting up. "Please? I just want this one thing."

Lily resisted helping her up. "And then your bucket list is finished?"

"My bucket list is complete when I'm dead." Grandma Dotty waved her hands more urgently.

Lily got to her feet and helped her grandmother to hers.

When she found her footing, Grandma Dotty kept hold of Lily's hands. "You have to ask Jud for me, Lily, even if it's through his agent. It shows you're over him. And when Jud performs at my birthday bash, he'll see that you're fine without him."

That wasn't true. None of it was true. Lily wasn't over him and she wasn't fine without him. There was an ache in her chest when she went to bed at night and when she got up in the morning. And then there was the heart-squeezing sadness when she thought of Jud singing or laughing or being kind to Grandma Dotty. He was such a good sport.

And a dirty, rotten rat.

But Grandma Dotty was right. Lily had to show Jud that the hurt he caused wasn't lasting.

Even if that was a lie.

12

The day of Grandma Dotty's birthday party dawned with clear blue skies at the Summer house in the Hamptons.

For many years, Grandma Dotty had headed south in the spring, or at the very latest, the summer. But lately, the family thought it was best that she stay in New York. This year, she was making the most of her birthday celebration. The guest list was bigger than ever.

Lily followed Kitty through the crowd. Lily hated crowds. But Kitty's short stature in no way prepared one for her take-charge nature. She cut a wide swath and smoothly swept past the bar, obtaining two glasses of prosecco, and then stopped in a far corner of the grand living room, which was large enough to play half-court basketball or to pack in seventy-five people standing up.

"Okay, spill, Lily." Kitty had big brown eyes that took note of every nuance, which was why she was such a good doctor. "I wasn't invited to Charleston with the rest of the pack, but that doesn't mean I don't love you enough to punish this out-of-line actor." Despite the cheer in Kitty's voice, her gaze caught on their youngest sister Maggie in a group with the rest of their sisters, and her expression turned sorrowful.

Kitty had meant well when she'd made Beck and Maggie aware that they didn't love each other as deeply as they should. She hadn't set out to fall in love with Maggie's fiancé later. Didn't matter. Maggie still blamed Kitty for the hurt and embarrassment she'd suffered from being jilted.

"They should have invited you to Charleston," Lily pointed out gently. She was working very hard at ignoring the group of performers on the far end of the living room where a small stage and sound system had been set up. But that didn't mean she hadn't seen Jud's dark head of hair in the midst of the group. "Maggie can't hold a grudge forever."

Kitty faced Lily, a resigned expression on her face. "She can and she will, and I won't begrudge her for it."

"You saved her from a sham of a marriage, Kitty. She'll realize that someday and be grateful." Lily sipped her prosecco. It was cool and crisp and reminded her of drinking with Jud on the yacht. She set it down on a small table.

"I hope someday Maggie's prince will come and she realizes the true depth of love. Maybe then she'll compare it to her feelings for Beck. Maybe then she'll accept my apology." Kitty drank half her glass of prosecco, which was unusual for her. "I can't seem to get on with my life without repairing this rift between us."

"Oh, no." Lily took Kitty by the shoulders. "Beck proposed?"

Kitty cringed, nodding.

"And you didn't accept."

Kitty shook her head and then drained her glass. "How can I? It feels like the ultimate betrayal to Maggie."

Lily picked up her abandoned prosecco and drank a

good slug of it. "That makes my personal woes seem meager by comparison."

The cast of *The Music Man* took the stage. They'd given Grandma Dotty a coveted spot in the chorus. As Jud took the stage, Kitty took Lily's hand. They stood side-by-side during the performance, smiling as if they weren't hurting inside.

I still love him.

"I like your dress," Lily told Kitty when the performance was over. It was either that or run for the hills before Jud made the rounds and she had to face him. "Pink always looks good on you."

Kitty wore a pink sundress. She tugged at the shoulder of Lily's bright blue, geometric sheath. "Blue was always your best color, but it shouldn't be your mood."

"I've been looking for you, Lily." Rachel appeared out of the crowd. She wore a deep green dress and dragged her father along behind her.

Kitty immediately inched closer to Lily and signaled to the waiter carrying a tray of fresh prosecco glasses. "Does anyone need a drink?"

Lily did. Despite that, she smiled and thanked Abe profusely for his donation to Hot Meals and Shelter.

"Daddy and I wanted to thank you, Lily." Rachel turned down the prosecco. "After things fell apart for me a few weeks ago, I took a good, long look at where I was headed. I consulted with Jud and Daddy, and we came up with a plan that benefits everyone."

Lily was certain that a stab of jealousy created frown lines on her forehead. "Are you going to have a role in Jud's movie?" It wasn't fair that Rachel should still be involved with Jud.

"No." It was Abe who answered. "After the wedding was

called off, Jud turned down my offer to help finance his film."

"He's not doing his film at all." Rachel's words were tinged with wonder, as if even she couldn't believe it.

Again, Lily was struck by jealousy. The Cohens knew more about Jud's life than she did.

As it should be.

Lily drew a calming breath. She had no claim on Jud. But she wondered why he'd turned his back on his dream.

"Instead of directing a theatrical film, Jud is producing a documentary about Rachel on his own shoestring budget." Abe rocked back on his heels. "We've been busy with it since Jud and Rachel returned to New York."

Jud and Rachel.

Lily wanted to crumble.

"*The Rediscovery of Rachel Cohen.*" Rachel pressed a kiss to her father's cheek. "Jud and his cameras are documenting my path back from being a villainous biotch to someone who can have meaningful relationships and a meaningful life. I'm in therapy and it's not a nightmare. Do you know that I love puppies? I've got two now and they're just so happy."

Lily didn't know what to say. She exchanged a glance with Kitty, whose mouth had dropped open.

Rachel wasn't stopping. "I owe you an apology, Lily. I was hurting and everything just got all twisted up inside of me. Everything that happened when we ran away was all my fault. I don't need to be the center of attention and put other people down to feel good." She paused to take a breath.

"And then there are puppies," Lily murmured.

"Exactly!" Rachel laughed. "You probably won't be surprised to hear that Paulo and I are dating again. We're in couples therapy, trying to connect with words this time. He's preparing to go away for the summer pro league and I'm learning Portuguese. We're taking things slowly. No more bridezilla!" Rachel grinned the way she had back in high school, back when she and Lily were friends.

"Isn't she awesome? I have my little girl back." Abe beamed. "You were part of that, Lily. If you ever need anything, just ask."

Lily vowed not to.

"Let's have lunch someday soon." Rachel dragged Abe off toward the buffet. "No cameras. I promise."

Lily and Kitty stood in silence. Lily was stunned. Across the room, Dotty and their father laughed.

"Do you ever wish you were closer with Dad?" Kitty's voice had a faraway quality to it, almost as if she weren't aware that she'd asked the question out loud.

"Sometimes," Lily allowed. It was hard to have a close relationship with their father when most days he seemed to care more about his mistresses than his wife or children. "Maybe Jud should shoot a documentary about Dad."

"Maybe he'd have a life-changing epiphany," Kitty said slowly.

They looked at each other for a few seconds before shaking their heads.

"Ladies and gentlemen." Jud's voice boomed out through the loudspeakers. "May I have your attention, please?"

"Is he..." Kitty rose up on her toes. "He's wearing that superhero suit."

Lily shook her head and pushed her glasses more firmly into place. "Grandma Dotty can talk a leopard into removing its spots." Or pay them to.

"This isn't part of our program today," Jud was saying. "Let me be clear. *No one* paid me to show up and wear my supersuit."

"Happy birthday to me!" Grandma Dotty shouted.

"I'm here to rescue Ms. Lily Summer." Jud pointed toward the back corner where Lily stood.

Her knees suddenly felt weak, and it had nothing to do with everyone's head swiveling in her direction.

"Could you come up here, Lily?"

"No," Lily whispered.

Kitty took both Lily's hands and gave them a good shake. "This is one of those moments, Lily. You need to look deep inside of you and figure out if your feelings for Judson Hambly are worth forgiving him for the hurt he caused you."

"What?" Lily blinked suddenly tear-filled eyes.

"He's looking at you the way Beck looks at me and the way Nino looks at Aubrey. He's looking at you like a man in love." Kitty had lowered her voice, but that didn't make her words any less urgent. "If you love him, Lily, you have to step off our safe little ledge back here and go to him."

"But everyone's watching." She shook her hands free and adjusted her glasses.

"He's a celebrity," Kitty said the obvious. "Everyone is always going to watch."

"Lily!" Grandma Dotty squirmed her way through the crowd. She was wearing what should have been her brides-maid dress for Rachel–a cream tank and silver skirt. "Marta brought me this dress this morning. Everyone's envious of my pockets." There was a bulge in her skirt where a pocket should be. Her flip phone? "Can you believe it? Jud is here in his superhero suit and calling your name."

"Lily Summer. Paging Lily Summer," Jud intoned from the other side of the large room. "Ladies and gentlemen, Lily is having a case of stage fright. Let's clear a path to make it easier for her to come up here."

Jud had superpowers for real. The crowd parted, creating an aisle for Lily to walk down.

"I should have worn a sexier dress," Lily mumbled.

"He'd still love you anyway." Grandma Dotty skipped ahead.

Love.

Lily knew that she loved Jud. But she found it hard to believe that he loved her. She kept putting one foot in front of the other anyway, trusting that each step might lead to something better.

"You know, I once told Lily that I only put this suit on for the cameras and if I'm paid." Jud commanded the room with his presence. "For the record, there are no cameras and although I was offered money to appear here today, I turned the offer down. That's how much Dotty and Lily Summer mean to me."

Lily passed Maggie, Aubrey, and Violet.

"Make sure that you're sure," Vi told her.

Was Lily sure of anything? Everything was turned upside down. Abe and Rachel. Rachel and Paulo. And now Jud and...Lily? Despite her doubts, despite her hurts, Lily was drawn to him all the same.

Jud's costume was silver and black with molded parts outlining where his very real six-pack abs were located. The supersuit alone was enough to mesmerize, that is, if you didn't look into Jud's amazing blue eyes. Whatever doubts Lily had carried with her on this long walk to the stage were soothed when she stared into his eyes. In them, she saw sincerity and love. So much love.

Jud extended a hand to help her onto the stage, lowering the microphone. "Was the suit too much?"

"No." Heaven willing, she was going to be telling her grandchildren about the moment when their grandfather won her back as Titanium Talon, superhero extraordinaire.

"The day I met Lily Summer, I was at a crossroads," Jud told the crowd, drawing her close to his side. "I didn't know it at the time. I only knew that things weren't working for me career-wise and that something had to change. I had a plan for that change, but it was a stupid plan." His gaze sought out Lily's. "I regret ever hatching that plan."

"Oh." One thing was clear, he still had the ability to melt her heart.

"What happened then?" Grandma Dotty was caught up in Jud's story.

Jud smiled at her grandmother as if he didn't mind the interruption. "And then I saw Lily, standing against a wall in the back of a large hotel ballroom. She was watching everyone else with a smile on her face that was part happy to be there and part sad to be there. I can't tell you how many events I've been to in my life where I was both glad to be on the guest list and weary that I'd come."

"You saw all that on my face?" Lily's cheeks heated.

Jud nodded. "And from the moment I stepped into Lily's world, I was in awe of her ability to stand up for herself and for others, to take a chance on trying something new, to trust a new group of friends, and then to draw a line when she felt an injustice had been done."

"Injustices plural," Lily murmured.

"Right," Jud agreed. "So many of us just go with the flow because it's difficult to step off the treadmill and reach for something different." Jud gazed down on Lily with so much love in his eyes that Lily thought she might cry. "To reach for *someone* different. Someone you didn't know you needed but suddenly realize you can't live without." Jud dropped to one knee. "At whatever pace love needs to grow."

And the crowd went wild–shouting, hooting, laughing. Phones came out. People stared.

Lily didn't care. Because the only person whose gaze mattered was Jud.

"Lily Summer, when you know, you know." Jud's smile was as tender and loving as his words. "My heart knows that I will never meet anyone else who can hold a candle to you. You make every day full of promise, every hour a joy, every minute full of love. I love you, Lily. I've loved you from the moment I set eyes on you. It just took my brain a bit longer to accept that fact."

Lily stared down at him, waiting for the proposal that she was certain would follow but all he did was smile up at her.

"Lily, this is where you reciprocate his love," Grandma Dotty whispered. Only she whispered loud enough for everyone to hear.

Laughter filled the room, but surprisingly, doubt didn't fill Lily's heart.

"When I came back from our little vacation," Lily began, squeezing Jud's hands. "I looked long and hard at all the negatives, all the hurts. I rewrote conversations in my head and second-guessed decisions I'd made. And then I made peace with all my actions. All except one. The fact that you weren't in my life anymore." She drew a deep breath, and this time Jud gave her hands a squeeze. "And just now, walking up to you, I decided that I need to do a better job trusting my instincts, especially when it comes to you. It wasn't that first kiss at the stroke of midnight that had me falling for you. It was those long, quiet conversations. Those moments when I shared my vulnerabilities, and you shared your doubts. Those were the times when I fell in love with you." When she realized he was just as human as she was.

Jud reached out a hand toward Grandma Dotty.

She dug into her skirt pocket and produced a small, Tiffany blue velvet box. "I was honored to be your sidekick today, Talon."

"Thank you, Daring Dotty." Jud opened the ring box, revealing a large diamond ring. But that diamond didn't shine as bright as the elation in his eyes. "The band is titanium. I hope you like it. I signed up for three more seasons as a superhero. I'm not ready to branch out into theatrical film just yet. I'm only beginning to spread my wings, honey. But it would make me one of the happiest, hardest working men alive if you'd do me the honor of becoming my wife. You can choose a date. Today, next month, next year, or five years from now. As long as we're together, you can set the pace."

"Are you sure?" Lily didn't want to rush things, despite the fact that her heart was singing a big, long note that sounded a lot like, *"YES!"*

"Am I sure that I want to be with you?" Jud nodded. "But I want you to be sure, too. As with all actors, my future isn't a straight line. My career may dip and dive. But I can take the lows and celebrate the highs as long as I know that you love me."

"I do love you." Lily recognized the love in her heart for what it was and let everyone know it with a shout of, *"I love Jud!"*

Her father washed a hand over his face.

"Then say yes, already." Grandma Dotty rapped her knuckles on the stage floor. "I've got an encore performance coming up."

"Yes. I'll marry you, Judson Hambly." And before Lily knew what was happening, Jud swept her into his arms and kissed her deeply, like this time it was for keeps.

EPILOGUE

Professor Violet Summer was happy with her life.

When she told that to her younger sister Maggie, who was a veterinarian and a jilted bride, Maggie laughed. They were behind their parents' Hamptons house for Lily's engagement party, walking toward the beach, each with a drink in hand. Maggie held a bottle of beer. Violet held a glass of sauvignon blanc. They sat down in the sand and stared at the ocean, squinting in the summer sun.

"We're the last two single sisters standing." Maggie sipped her beer. "We need to stand together."

"I'm not looking for a man to complete me," Vi told her. "I have research projects to conduct, papers to write, a name to make for myself."

"Is that all? I'm looking for a man to take to Kitty's wedding." Maggie removed her sandals and pushed her bare feet in the sand. "You know their engagement is inevitable. And since I used to be engaged to Kitty's groom, I need someone *extra*."

Vi sipped her wine as a particularly loud wave crashed on the shore. She wore a blue silk tank top and sand-colored linen slacks but was wishing she was in shorts and a cotton T-shirt. "Extra what?"

"I don't know. Rich, handsome, royal." Maggie laughed. "That's it. I want my own Prince Charming."

Yikes, this could be bad. "Are you serious? Princes are hard to come by, Maggie. We get a few at Harvard." But a very few and from such small kingdoms that a royal title was a bit sketchy.

"Get out." Maggie bumped her shoulder against Violet's. "Can you introduce me to one?"

She was serious.

"No. I don't want to get in the matchmaking business. Remember me? Professor at Harvard?" Vi was certain matchmaking by the staff was frowned upon.

"Come on. One prince. For me. Please?" Maggie set her beer in the sand, laced her fingers, and propped her chin on her digits.

There was one man who might fit the bill, but Violet would have to approach the task very carefully.

"Excuse me, ladies." A cowboy stood in front of them. Tall, muscular, wide brimmed hat. His tan cowboy boots were half buried in the sand. "Have you seen a white horse in the past five minutes?"

Violet blinked. She leaned closer to Maggie. "I think I've had too much to drink, Mags. I'm seeing things. Specifically, a tall, sexy cowboy with kissable lips."

Maggie shaded her eyes with one hand. "I'm in the same boat. I'm seeing the same mirage. It's got to be a hallucination. We don't get cowboys in the Hamptons."

Horses hooves thundered toward them from behind them.

"Never mind. I see her." The cowboy walked around behind them and whistled shrilly. "Tally ho!"

"I'm so confused. Now the cowboy is calling out the fox hunt?" Violet got to her feet. "Are you sure I'm not hallucinating?"

"We're sharing the same vision." Maggie got to her feet.

They both turned just as a white horse skidded to a halt, practically landing on her haunches and sending a wave of sand toward Violet and Maggie.

The cowboy didn't move a muscle other than to hold out an apple slice. "Good girl, Tally. Easy now."

The mare's white nostrils flared. Refusing the treat, she jerked her head to look at Vi and Maggie.

"You want a slice of apple, don't you, girl," the cowboy said in a sultry voice that tugged at something deep in Violet's chest. "You want it more than you want to trample me or these pretty ladies."

Violet gasped. Unlike Maggie, who was a large animal veterinarian, Vi wasn't used to being around anything larger than a golden retriever.

"I'm just kidding." The cowboy gave Vi a look over his shoulder that made her pulse pound like crazy. "Tally's as gentle as a kitten, aren't you, honey?" His voice was deep and rich with a slight Texas twang.

The mare took a step closer to him, then another.

Violet had definitely had too much to drink because that voice called to her the same way it called to that horse of his. She took a step closer. And then another.

In one smooth movement, the cowboy leapt onto the mare's back–no saddle, no reins, no halter.

"Oh." He was hot, hotter than Lily's fiancé actor Judson Hambly. "*Oh*," Vi said again but dreamily this time because it seemed required.

"Thanks for your help, ma'ams." The cowboy extended a hand toward Vi, as if for a shake.

Violet eyed that hand. Handshakes were rarer now that the world had been through a pandemic. "I didn't do anything."

"You didn't run screaming, which would have made Tally bolt to Sag Harbor." His hand was still extended.

Vi took it, momentarily losing herself in his large clasp and the heat of his skin.

Oh, yeah. Fantasy time.

"To properly thank you, let's go for a ride." Without warning, the cowboy swung her up behind him, let out one of those cowboy cries, and the horse galloped across the beach leaving Violet's wine and sister behind them.

Want to find out what happens next?

Follow Melinda Curtis on Amazon to be notified of the release of Violet's story: *When You Kiss Me.*

Did you read A Kiss is Just a Kiss, the first book in the Kissing Test series?

Did you read And Then He Kissed Me, the second book in the Kissing Test series?

ALSO BY MELINDA CURTIS

Other Series by Melinda Curtis you may enjoy:

Sunshine Valley – *Poker playing widows give Cupid a hand in small town Sunshine!*

Mountain Monroes – *They inherited a small town in Idaho! Now what!*

Bridesmaids Novellas – *A funny thing happened as bridesmaids count down to the wedding!*

Melinda Curtis is the *USA Today* bestselling author of light-hearted contemporary romance. In addition to her independent books, including the Kissing Test series, she's published with Grand Central Forever and Harlequin, including her book *Dandelion Wishes*, which is now a TV movie – *Love in Harmony Valley*, starring Amber Marshall.

Melinda and her husband recently moved to a "fixer" in Oregon's Willamette Valley. When not writing, Melinda can be found reading or plotting books, making a bucket list or potting plants. She enjoys writing comedy into books about kissing and hopes readers enjoy them enough to come back for more!